I0685241

Die a Yellow Ribbon

Pecan Bayou, Volume 9

Teresa Trent

Published by Teresa Trent, 2020.

This is a work of fiction. Similarities to real people, places, or events are entirely coincidental.

DIE A YELLOW RIBBON

First edition. July 13, 2020.

Copyright © 2020 Teresa Trent.

ISBN: 978-1732946835

Written by Teresa Trent.

Chapter 1

My head was full of tidying tips, and I had complete, albeit misguided, confidence that I could tidy any place.
Marie Kondo

"Wait a minute, wait a minute! You can't do that. I have press immunity." Rocky stood toe-to-toe with Belinda Donaldson, Pecan Bayou's formidable meter maid. I suppose these days she's known as a parking attendant, but in a little town like Pecan Bayou, Texas, she's still a meter maid to us.

Belinda looked up from her ticket book and raised an eyebrow. "Press immunity? Did you just make that up? You never cease to amaze me with your creative mind, Rocky. Especially when I read that so-called newspaper of yours."

"You, my lady, are only here because Mayor Obermeyer is too stubborn to install parking meters. You and your tire marking are antiquated."

"Sticks and stones, paper man. You didn't just move here yesterday. You know you're allowed one-hour parking in the downtown area, and it doesn't matter if a machine tells you or I do. You, Ruby Green, and especially that dude from the vitamin store—you all act like you have carte blanche with your parking space around here."

"This is where we work. We should be able to park for free."

"Tell it to the judge." She ripped off a ticket and handed it to Rocky in a crisp fashion. "Press immunity, my foot. Have a nice day."

Belinda turned with a whirl. Her long ponytail was secured with a beautiful custom-knitted scrunchie made of various

1

colors of yarn and accented with beads that clicked as she made her rather dramatic exit. I had never seen anything like it.

Rocky grumbled and entered the offices of the Pecan Bayou Gazette. I had watched and heard the entire scene through the window instead of working on my latest helpful hints article that was due shortly.

"She got you again," I said as Rocky continued to fume.

"Mayor Obermeyer is out of his head. Doesn't he know we're trying to encourage people to shop in the downtown area, not discourage them? I'm telling you, his stubbornness will be the death of retail in Pecan Bayou." Rocky slapped his hand down on the ad section of the Gazette. "I barely have enough ads to fill the page. That mall outside of Andersonville is killing us. Next thing we know the shops will be closing down and Pecan Bayou will become a ghost town."

"But doesn't the mall advertise?" I asked. Rocky had always seemed like a glass-half-full kind of guy. He had to be, seeing as he had endured running a small-town newspaper for years and still kept it afloat in an age where people reached for their morning news online instead of from under the bush where the newsboy throws it.

"Betsy, you may be the world's smartest helpful hints columnist, but when it comes to advertising, you're out of your league. Most of the mall's advertising dollars are going to the Andersonville weekly paper or the web. We've been cut out. Pecan Bayou is full of wonderful shopping treasures, and yet people are willing to drive twenty miles to get a piece of greasy food-court pizza and mill around overpriced stores."

A wave of guilt rushed through me. I loved to shop at the mall, although it could get expensive with three children to outfit. "We were just there this weekend. The boys needed new shoes. It seems we buy a pair, and before we know it, they've outgrown them. I planned to do some shopping for myself, but do you know how much they want for a handbag over there?"

"Exactly. Handbags, shoes, greasy pizza. You should keep your loyalty and your shopping dollars right here in Pecan Bayou. There's absolutely no reason to be taking your money there—you can find everything you need right here." Rocky settled himself behind his cluttered desk, tossing the ticket onto a pile of other unpaid tickets.

As much as I wanted to agree with him, I knew I couldn't. Pecan Bayou's clothing stores were a little dated. If my style was vintage 1995 or the latest in hunter camouflage, sure, I'd keep my shopping dollars here. But I do enjoy an occasional up-to-date fashion. "Come on, Rocky. Be serious. Have you tried to get advertising from the mall?"

"Of course, but they think we're too small and our ad rates too high. Can you believe that? People look to this paper for the latest news catered to them and their community. Those needle-nosed millennials at the mall know nothing at all about the power of good, old-fashioned advertising."

"That's too bad, but you have to admit, relative to the size of the state, we're tiny."

"I can't believe I'm going to say this, but this year I'm looking forward to the unabated greed of the Golden Pecan Treasure Hunt. At least we'll have people walking around downtown again. Some days it feels like people only use downtown as the landing strip for the coffee shop while they're on their way to something better."

"Yeah, well, if they ever put a Starbucks in this town, Earl Brown can kiss his monopoly on coffee goodbye."

"Not exactly a monopoly," Rocky argued. "Birdie's Diner makes a decent cup of joe. I can't believe she's decided to close during the treasure hunt. Why she would take a gamble on the golden pecan and give up the money she could make from a large crowd of hungry, thirsty people is beyond me."

I glanced out at the main street of Pecan Bayou. "I guess Benny's Barbecue will be at capacity."

"He sure will be." Rocky stared out the window, his brow furrowing. "What if people don't consider the treasure hunt a worthwhile pursuit this year? What if they're too busy ordering stuff online and traveling to bigger towns?"

"That'll never happen, Rocky. Nobody turns away free money."

"I guess you're right. This gold-crazed day has been going on since the 1930s as a cure to the depression."

I remembered learning the story in elementary school. It almost sounded like a fairy tale at the time, what with golden pecans and hidden treasure. "The mayor back then...oh, what was his name?"

"Phinneus Lincoln," Rocky responded sounding as if I had been studying for a test.

"Right. Do I remember the story correctly? Phinneaus Lincoln made a speech in front of the city council wishing the yearly pecan crop could be of gold and after that famous speech, his wife, a beloved elementary school teacher, had her third graders make the first golden pecan? Wasn't it made of paper mache and gold paint?"

"Yep, one of the Pecan Bayou traditions people are still loyal to although now we make it out of an oversized plastic Easter egg," Rocky said.

The sound of metal crunching on concrete hit our ears—someone was outside. Rocky and I were the only ones at the office today, his son being smart enough to get out of town before the golden pecan hunt kicked off. "Is Nicholas here?" I asked. "I thought he was off visiting his girlfriend."

We went out the back door that opened onto an alley to find Bunny Donaldson with her hand in a dented metal trashcan. Bunny was the sister of Belinda the meter maid. She too wore her long hair pulled back, and at the moment, Bunny's long, blonde braid dipped dangerously close to a sticky mess left from a paper plate covered in red barbecue sauce.

"What the hell are you doing, Bunny?" Rocky shouted. "Can't you see this is private property? Those things don't belong to you. I should call the police."

"These things are no longer yours once you deposit them in an outside waste can. Read the law, Rocky. Read the law." As the owner of Sprouting Serenity, Bunny called herself an environmentalist, which to her meant if it was in her environment, she was free to take it and "recycle" it as she saw fit. She was the town dumpster diver, turning everyone else's trash into her treasure.

Bunny pointed at us, her bony finger protruding from a fingerless white lace glove, her braid swinging out from under her sun hat. "This is a discard receptacle, which makes it public domain. I can dig all I want. Look at all the aluminum cans in here. Why aren't you recycling these? Do you think this planet is going to last forever?"

"As a matter of fact, I do, but in the interest of sustaining the planet, I'll be happy to share my cans with you if you clean up this mess then get out of here. Do you hear?" Rocky harrumphed.

"I hear you. Hold on. I have a little more shopping to do."

"You're not shopping. You're dumpster diving."

"I beg your pardon. You're too cheap to get a dumpster. What's the date stamp on this can? 1955? No one has metal trash cans anymore. I'll give you credit, though, at least it's not made of plastic. Mark my words, plastic will surely be the end of us all. It's from the devil, I tell you."

"Then you should congratulate me for not polluting the planet with yet another green plastic trash receptacle." Rocky took a bow.

"Hmm," Bunny mumbled as she pulled out a piece of discarded paper. "You people only print on one side of the paper? That is so irresponsible. Reuse. Recycle!"

Rocky's mouth hung open. Bunny was on a roll. I felt like I needed to step in before this turned into an alley brawl. "Bunny," I said, "I'm sure you're looking forward to the treasure hunt. You're obviously very good at searching out things."

"Oh, you mean that chemical-filled plastic pecan, made all pretty and shiny with toxic paints, that the chamber of commerce drags out every year? Now that Vic Butler is the head of the chamber with that bimbo wife of his, you can bet the whole thing is even more shady. That man is too smooth."

Rocky tipped his head back. "What do you have against Vic and Sarah?"

Bunny stiffened. "She might have been in the running for Miss Texas, but Sarah Butler is evil. Oh, she looks all beautiful on the outside, thanks to all that fake plastic. But on the inside that girl is a rotted piece of fruit. Someday she'll pay for what she's done."

"What the hell are you talking about, Bunny? Did you eat some of that old potato salad from the diner?" Rocky asked.

"None of your business. If you don't mind, I choose to refrain from talking to the media."

Rocky shrugged. "Whatever. Just clean up this mess before you leave."

Bunny turned away and started transferring the crumpled soda cans into a burlap bag.

"What was that all about?" I asked as we re-entered the newspaper office.

"Who knows. Better yet, who cares? Now about that article you're supposed to be writing on turning plastic bags into throw rugs. Bunny's sure to love that one." Rocky winked.

"I'm getting to it, boss. First, I want to finish my series on organization."

"More articles on sorting the sock drawer? Really, Betsy. This town can only take so many 'roll your socks' articles. Change it up a little bit."

How could he not understand how much Marie Kondo and her book, *Tidying Up,* had changed my life? My home used to be chaotic and a revolving pile of dirty laundry. With three kids, I was finding it almost impossible to keep things in order. Marie restored my sanity. I needed to shout her message from the highest mountaintop, and luckily, I had a platform to do just that!

Rocky still stood at my desk, expecting an answer.

"Okay. This article is the last one. I promise."

"Good."

As I turned back to my computer, I heard Bunny still clanking cans in the alley. I couldn't stop thinking about how much Bunny's face changed the minute we mentioned Sarah Butler. She was beautiful, but I'd never seen anything in her that hinted at evil.

"Excuse me." Mark Valencia, a new store owner in Pecan Bayou, stood at the front counter. Mark's muscles bulged impressively under a royal blue polo emblazoned with the words "Maximum Muscle" on the chest.

"Yes, can I help you?" I asked.

Mark took a folder from under his arm. "Yes, I'd like to buy an ad in your paper."

Rocky rose from his desk and greeted Mark with an enthusiastic smile. Small-town newspapers didn't survive on subscriptions alone. Advertising was an angel from heaven.

"Of course, what did you have in mind?" Rocky said.

"I'm the owner of Maximum Muscle. Maybe you've seen it?"

I'd certainly seen it. Both of my boys had been bugging us to take them there. Maximum Muscle sold powdered mixes and supplements that claimed the user would turn into a weightlifter with large biceps and six-pack abs. His little store was quite busy, especially after the high school wrestling team got wind of it.

"Yes, and I should have stopped by sooner to say welcome to the community." Rocky extended his hand. "I'm Rocky Whitson, editor of the Pecan Bayou Gazette."

Mark flashed a winning smile toward Rocky. "Mark Valencia, nice to meet you. No big deal. I find most of the real men in town get over to my store eventually. I have a complete line of senior supplements."

Rocky's expression soured. "Great. When I find a senior, I'll send them on over."

Mark gave him a wink. "Don't wait too long. Muscles can atrophy in just a few years." He looked back at the street. "Was that Bunny Donaldson coming from the alley? Does she come dig through your trash cans? I can't keep that woman out of the can behind my store. What is the deal with her? She called me the devil the other day. That Donaldson woman could use a mental health check."

"She probably called you a devil because you're both in the same business."

"She sells bodybuilding supplements?" He put a hand on his chin and glanced out at the street.

"She owns our local health food store. Unless you have organic, free-range, and pure stamped on those vitamins you sell, she wouldn't touch them." I had never thought about it before now, but Rocky was right. Bunny and Mark were competing for the business of people wanting to lead healthier lives, but their ideologies were at odds.

"Great. Just what I needed. Next time Bunny calls me names, I'll make sure she thinks twice. No wo... No person has the right to treat me like that."

Three strikes for Bunny. Not only did he dislike her because she was in the natural foods business and digging through his trashcans, but he wasn't all that crazy about the fact she was a woman. "Well, Bunny has had a hard time of it lately. She had a death in the family."

Mark nodded. "That's too bad, but that doesn't mean she can take it out on me. Do you know she threw eggs at my window last week?"

"No doubt, cage-free," Rocky said.

"I don't care what they are, she needs to back off. I haven't called the police yet, but one more stunt and I'm going to the cops. The woman's a menace. As far as I'm concerned, she can take her herbs and eggs and stuff them up her—"

Rocky cleared his throat, cutting Mark off. "What kind of ad are you interested in?"

Mark regained his composure. "I'm not sure. Do you have a rate sheet?"

"We sure do," Rocky said, glee in his voice. "Let me get a copy for you from the back. Stay right there!"

Mark smiled at me, and then the grinding of heavy metal music filled the room. He fished a phone out of his pocket and tapped the screen.

"Mark here. Yes...no. I said I wanted it today. Get me? Today or maybe somebody would like to know what you're up to...get me?" The anger in his voice was escalating, but he toned it down when his gaze came back to me.

"Uh...thank you for calling." He clicked off the phone.

I smiled back a little uncomfortably. "Business problems?"

"Yeah. You know..." He shrugged and glanced away.

Rocky returned with a laminated rate sheet in his hand. "Now, let's get you an ad in the paper, Mark."

As Mark and Rocky started working on the ad, I decided Bunny's cause had inspired me, and I would switch to my article on recycling plastic grocery bags. I started to type at my computer, explaining the process of converting bags into strips when Rocky finished up with Mark and returned to his desk.

"Have you ever thought of Sarah Butler as evil?" I asked.

"No. How could a beauty queen be evil? I don't think she ever won Miss Congeniality. I mean, she keeps to herself, but I don't see her as evil. If anything, she brightens up a room. Now I'm sure other people in town have different opinions about her. It's hard to be so perfect around here."

"First of all, yes, beauty queens can be bad. Beauty pageants are a competition like any other, which can bring out the worst in some people. She always seemed friendly enough to me, though."

"Who knows. People talk. And I wouldn't put too much stock in what our resident eco-terrorist is saying. Bunny has always had what my grandmother would have called flights of fancy. I think she's a clear victim of too much granola. All that fiber can kill a person. That's why God invented bacon and eggs."

"I guess."

Rocky held up a softball-sized pecan coated with gold paint. "So, who do you think will find the golden pecan this year?"

"I don't know, but you'd better hide it better than the year you hid it in a tree. This year's prize is pretty impressive."

Libby Loper, who ran a successful dude ranch on the edge of town, donated the grand prize this year, a seven-day cruise leaving out of Galveston. Sun, fun, and a vacation Leo and I desperately needed.

"Okay. Maybe it was a bad idea to stick it in the Christmas tree."

Rocky was referring to the giant pine near the town square we used for a Christmas tree each year. Even without the lights and decorations, it was still called the Christmas tree.

"It was the shortest treasure hunt in the history of Pecan Bayou," I laughed. "People didn't need to follow the clues. They just had to look up, and there it was."

Rocky held up a hand. "I accept the blame on that one, but this year, by tying in our failing downtown stores, it's a win-win."

"So, where are you going to hide it?"

Rocky's eyes widened. "And why would I tell you? Last I heard you've already started packing for that cruise. I'd better not find out you're shopping for beachwear at the mall."

"Then maybe you can tell *me*?" My stepson Tyler entered from the street lugging in two cases of bottled water on a dolly.

"This is a surprise," I said. Out for summer break, I hadn't seen Tyler get off the couch this early in the day since the last school bell rang.

"Mr. Butler from the bank called me and asked if I would unload some items for the treasure hunt. He got a discount on a giant order and they parked it all in the alley behind Benny's Barbecue. I guess he was planning ahead for hurricane season. He wants you guys to store these cases here."

"Sure," Rocky said, then turned to me. "And as for your request on the whereabouts of the golden pecan, no one gets to know but me. You'd have to use torture to get it out of me." Rocky, ever the dramatic, feigned victimhood with the back of his hand melodramatically stuck to his forehead.

I gave him a crosswise glance. "My boss. The world master of hyperbole."

"Where do you want these?" Tyler asked.

"Comes in handy in the newspaper business, Betsy." He focused on the cases of water bottles. "Just set them in the back." Rocky placed his hands on my shoulders. "You have an article to finish, young lady. I already have two writers late on their deadlines. The whole town is waiting for the bowling scores from Lester, so I can't disappoint them further with a missing Happy Hinter article. Besides, I need to think. Use the old gray matter." He tapped his temple and walked away.

I returned to my computer screen and said to the retreating Rocky, "Yeah, try to think of where to hide the golden pecan that isn't so obvious."

"Not a problem. I figured that out weeks ago," Rocky answered with a twinkle in his eye.

Chapter 2

After visiting with Rocky and finishing my article on recycling plastic bags, I decided to pay a visit to my father over at the Pecan Bayou police station. I was worried about him trying to get ready for the Pecan Bayou Golden Pecan Treasure Hunt, especially after what had happened last year. A few of our less reputable citizens had imbibed before the hunt, and there was an all-out brawl in front of Birdie's Diner. This year my father planned to set up a perimeter of volunteer deputies to help keep the peace among the treasure hunters. His next problem was trying to get said volunteers. Everybody in town wanted to find that golden pecan.

As I walked into the one-story tan brick police department that felt like a second home to me, I found my father looking over the shoulder of Mrs. Thatcher, our dispatcher, pointing to the computer screen. This tableau of the two of them set up against the deep brown 1970s paneling was forever locked in my memories.

"So, if you calculate the area we have to cover, this is going to spread us pretty thin," my father said.

"Real thin. Plus, we have to put Beckwith in here to cover the phones." She nodded to George Beckwith, who was eating a submarine sandwich in the back room while watching something on his cell phone.

My father heaved a sigh. Mrs. Thatcher was his most valuable and most consistent coworker. "And there's no way I can change your mind on that?"

Mrs. Thatcher lowered her bifocals. "Not a chance. My husband, Josiah, and I have been planning to do the hunt together this year. Besides that, even though he's been studying past treasure hunts like a history major before finals, he can't even find his socks in the morning. We never had a cruise offered before. You think I'm going to trust something as important as this to him alone?"

My dad patted her shoulder. "And you deserve it. I'm just worried that we'll have a brawl start again. Years and years of driving around rescuing people's cats and making sure that their neighbors' TVs are turned down on summer nights must not count for much."

"Not when you're talking seven days of fun and sun starting from glorious Galveston." She made her rhyme sing at the end like a commercial on KNUT, home of the nuttiest country music in Texas.

"Good morning, Dad," I said.

"Morning, Betsy." His eyebrows rose slightly. "You wouldn't want to volunteer to be my deputy, would you?"

"Not really."

"How about that husband of yours?"

"I don't know how formidable a weatherman would be. Besides, we want to hunt for the pecan. The kids do, too. What about Art Rivera?"

"Art is giving up his duties as coroner for the weekend and going on a fishing trip without me. Meanwhile, I'll be keeping myself busy making sure the fools of Pecan Bayou don't conk each other over the head when they find that stupid plastic pecan. Now our lovely dispatcher here tells me she and her husband are leaving me to join the fray."

"I don't think you understand the seriousness of the situation, Judd," Mrs. Thatcher said. "Now that the prize is a cruise, Josiah has taken the spare bedroom as his command center. He has flowcharts, street maps with pins in them, and strategies typed up on his computer. It's more than a cruise to him. He thinks of it as his job now that he's retired. A reason to get up in the morning."

"Well, I appreciate a man with a plan. I just wish I had a better one." Dad ran a hand through his salt-and-pepper hair, leaving a few strands sticking up on top.

"Excuse me." The president of Pecan Bayou's only bank, Vic Butler, had quietly walked in behind me. "Good morning, all," he said in a booming voice. Vic was well-loved in our town, not only as a former rodeo cowboy but when a rancher needed a loan, he was willing to give them a listen. "Sorry to interrupt. Glad to hear you talking about our treasured golden pecan."

My father reached out and shook Vic's hand. "If you're here to check out the security, I have bad news, Vic. Our workforce will be running very thin on the night of the treasure hunt. I don't know if we will have anybody in the early morning hours."

Pecan Bayou's fun family event was ridiculously long and went on for twenty-four hours, putting a strain on even the strongest families. Rocky had become so adept at hiding that little plastic pecan (with the exception of the Christmas tree year) that sometimes it took an entire day to find it. We even had a year where no one found it, and they had to put everybody's names in a bag and draw for the prize. A well-hidden golden pecan meant there could be people wandering around the streets of Pecan Bayou at two and three in the morning. Then there would also be the people who had just come out of the bar, who were not so much as wandering around as stumbling.

"I have complete confidence in you, Judd, but I'm actually here about something else. Could you tell me how one takes out a restraining order?"

Mrs. Thatcher tilted her head slightly. "Is somebody bothering you, Vic?"

"It's a little embarrassing," he stammered.

"Would you like to go into my office and tell me?" my father urged.

He sighed. "At this point it seems like a wasted effort. You all might know already. It's not for me. It's for my wife. Bunny Donaldson keeps hounding her."

Now this was beginning to ring a bell. Rocky and I had just listened to Bunny rant about how much she hated Sarah Butler.

"How is she bothering her? Is she making threats? Do you feel like Sarah isn't safe or that Bunny might commit physical violence against your wife?"

"I'm not sure. Bunny is making life miserable for my sweet Sarah. She keeps accusing her of terrible things. That crazy woman makes her sound like a trollop. I'm afraid people will start to believe her."

My father crossed his arms and tapped his chin. "I can keep Bunny away from her, but I can't keep her quiet. Even if we did get a restraining order, she could still go around town bad-mouthing her. Is there any chance her comments would qualify as slander?"

Vic paused for a moment. "My job is to bring in commerce to the town, and I'll admit, I don't always succeed. People don't always like me when I can't give them a loan, and they don't mince words about it, but when it comes to my Sarah, it's different. With the mall pulling sales away from downtown, my position at the chamber may be precarious. They only gave me that job because I'm also president of the bank. Sometimes I wonder if our citizens might want more of a go-getter kind of person."

My father rested his hands on his police belt. "I'll keep an eye on Bunny and have a few words with her about what she's been doing. That can be our first step toward keeping the peace."

"Thanks. I'd appreciate that. You can see how difficult this is."

"Well, Bunny has never been right since her sister died. I think we've all tried to cut her some slack because of that. Such a strange accident."

"I suppose you're right," Vic said as he began to back out of the office. "Thanks. Sometimes we think we are all living in Mayberry, but that's a myth. People like Bunny do seem to keep us grounded."

I glanced at my phone. I needed to get back. "I'd better get going. I just dropped by to say hello. Don't let all this golden pecan stuff wear you out, Dad." I grabbed my bag to leave.

"No more than it usually does."

As I strolled down the street, I spotted Mark Valencia standing outside Maximum Muscle. Next to him was a man even bigger than Mark, with his hand planted firmly on the fitness store owner's shoulder. I slowed down but could easily overhear their conversation.

"I don't care what you think," Mark said. "I'm not paying that price. What you sell is garbage compared to what I'm shipping in from San Antonio. Face it. Our little working relationship has come to a sad and sorry end."

"You can't mean that. I have an entire shipment of the stuff I have to pay for. You made a promise."

"Only a verbal agreement."

"I don't care what you call it. You broke your word." Big man's face was reddening.

"Sorry. I guess I don't know what came over me. Oh wait, I do know. A better deal." Mark smirked at the angry man. Would they begin a fight right there in the street? I backed up, ready to return to the police station if need be.

Instead, the bigger man cursed and stomped down the street. Mark Valencia straightened his shirt and darted into his store.

We were experiencing a record-breaking heatwave this summer, and between this encounter and Bunny Donaldson threatening Sarah, tempers were rising as fast as the thermometer.

Chapter 3

"A restraining order against Bunny? She seems pretty harmless to me." Aunt Maggie placed a plate of freshly baked cookies in front of me. "Try these. I just got the recipe from Libby."

I took a bite, and a mixture of pecan and cream cheese played on my tongue. "These are delicious. What are they called?"

"Cheesecake cookies. I think I'll send some to Danny's day habilitation center. They love any excuse for a party over there."

My cousin Danny grabbed a cookie. "Don't take them all to day hab, Mama. I might not get enough."

"You've already had enough, baby," Maggie answered.

I reached for a second cookie. "Vic said Bunny is saying terrible things about Sarah, but he didn't go into much detail."

Maggie scowled. "Well, I'm not one to gossip—"

"Gossip is the devil's telephone," Danny said in rote fashion. He'd heard that cautionary warning before.

"You are so right." Maggie smiled at Danny then turned back to me. "But I heard Sarah was very seductive."

"How seductive?" I asked.

"Very." Maggie winked.

"Very." Danny repeated and winked. I doubted my cousin understood what seductive meant, but he was never one to be left out of a conversation.

Maggie blew out a sigh and changed the subject. "I tell you, with all of this insanity going on about finding that golden pecan I almost want to sit back and watch everybody else run around after the fool thing. Ruby is fairly driving me crazy. She says she has a battle plan of some sort."

Ruby had a battle plan, and Josiah Thatcher had built a Pecan Bayou Golden Pecan command center. People seemed to be going all-out this year.

"Do you think Ruby would mind if I let her have all the fun and I stayed home in the air conditioning?" Maggie asked. "Besides that, Danny doesn't have anywhere to go that day. His center for disabled adults isn't open on Saturday."

"We are talking about the same woman, aren't we? The last time Ruby cut my hair she talked the whole time about the cruise the two of you would be going on if you won. Something about the two most eligible ladies hooking up with some cruise ship Romeos?"

Maggie smiled and shook her head. "Yes. She said that to me too, and then she explained what hooking up meant."

"I'm glad she did. I sure didn't want to explain it to you," I said.

"Baby girl, I've been around a while. I might not know the current terminology, but I still know what Ruby had in mind. Not sure I'm crazy about the new term—makes the act of a man and woman becoming intimate sound like Velcro."

"And what would you do if you found the golden pecan and won the cruise?"

Maggie laughed and pushed Danny's hand away from the plate. "I don't rightly know. I know that there's the option of cashing it out, and as much as I used to watch *The Love Boat*, I would probably take the cash. It's always a good idea to pad your retirement account."

"Mama. We need to go on the boat," Danny said.

"You don't like boats. You don't like being on the water. When Uncle Judd took you fishing, you pestered him until he put you back on dry land."

"But I would like it this time."

"Yoo-hoo." Ruby Green stuck her head through the unlocked door. Normally, Aunt Maggie would have the door open and the breeze coming through the screen door, but today the only thing that was creeping in was the insufferable heat. "Anybody home?"

Ruby was our town's beautician, and because she lived her life helping other people look beautiful, or in some cases merely passable, she applied her talents to creating some very individual looks on herself. Today she was decked out in a frog theme with a silk frog-patterned scarf highlighting a lime green tailored shirt and green striped capri pants. Tiny frogs dangled from her ears, and they bounced each time she moved, making me think of Mark Twain's famous story "The Celebrated Jumping Frog of Calaveras County."

"Aren't you usually at the salon this time of day?" I asked. The Best Little Hairhouse in Texas was the most popular salon in town since it was the only beauty parlor within a thirty-mile radius.

"Nah. Business is slow. People don't have their minds on hairdos right now. We're all plotting for a way to get that gold pecan. I closed down for the day. In search of a bigger financial nut, you might say. Today we're meeting to finalize on a foolproof plan to find the prize. Maggie and I are going to go on this cruise together and check out the singles scene down in *Me-hee-co*."

Aunt Maggie pushed at the air with her hand. "Go on with yourself, Ruby. I have no desire whatsoever to check out the singles scene. I'm long past that. There's no replacing the love of my life, God rest his soul, so I don't even want to try."

"And that's where you're making a mistake," Ruby said. "Look at you. You're young. You're vibrant. You deserve to have a life. You can't wear those widow's weeds forever."

"I think you've sucked in too much Final Net. Didn't they teach you in that beauty school not to inhale? Besides that, what man is going to want to date either of us? We aren't sexy chicks hanging out on the lido deck in our polka-dot bikinis. Now, if the singles' scene is at the bingo table between the polyester grandmas and Botox divorcees, we'd at least get some attention."

Ruby didn't flinch. "You'd be surprised at my allure. Why, I caught Lester Jibbets giving me the eye in church last week."

"It's called astigmatism."

"Nevertheless, there was contact made of the flirting kind."

"And what would you do if Lester actually asked you out?" Maggie asked.

"Ooh." Ruby looked appalled. "I hadn't thought of that. The fun is in the chase, not the capture."

"Exactly. So what in the world would we be doing on a cruise? Yes, I'm alone, but I'm not lonely. I'm happy. I'm not looking for a new man in my life."

"She has a man in her life," Danny professed.

"That's right," Maggie agreed.

"I don't mean like that, Danny." Ruby tugged at her silk scarf, looking discouraged. I loved Ruby and her outlook on life. She was always in the middle of sparking joy, and Aunt Maggie was seriously raining on her parade.

"I think it's a fine idea," I said in my most encouraging voice. "If you want to go on a cruise, then why not? I know you'll have fun."

Ruby perked up a little bit. "Thank you. At least there are some members of your family who have their heads on their shoulders. I knew I could always count on you to see things realistically, Betsy. But enough about me. We need to talk about how we will be the victors in finding the golden pecan."

"About that," Maggie said. "I may not be able to help you out with it."

"What do you mean?" Ruby was clearly taken aback. "We had a plan. I don't think I can execute this without you."

"Danny's center is closed on Saturday, so we'll have him along."

"That's okay. The more, the merrier, right, Danny?"

Danny gave an infectious grin and pumped his fist in the air. "Right!"

"Nevertheless, he can get us distracted."

"Lighten up, Maggie. It will be fun! I was thinking about this last night, and I decided I've been going about it all wrong. When I've done this in other years, I wracked my brain thinking about the best place to hide something, but I was always thinking about it from *my* perspective. This year I had an epiphany."

"Pray tell what?" Maggie shooed Danny's hand away from his fourth helping of cookies.

"I need to think like Rocky."

Thinking like Rocky was something that would be extremely hard for Ruby. She had her own take on the world, which involved fashion, hair, and gossip. Rocky was more current events, sports, and...gossip. Maybe she *could* get insight into him.

"And how do you propose to do that?" I asked.

Ruby switched her focus from my aunt to me. "Why through you, of course."

Her gaze intensified as she gave me a smile that would make the Cheshire Cat wince. I placed a hand on my throat. "Me?"

"Yes. You. You are the inside track to the Pecan Bayou Gazette and all its doings. Who else works with Rocky and knows his every thought?"

"His son, Nicholas?"

"Yes, I suppose so," she agreed. "But I don't have the access to Nicholas that I have to you. Tell me, because I'm sure all you newsies know. Where is Rocky going to hide the golden pecan?"

My mouth dropped at her blatant question. "Even if I did know, I wouldn't tell you. It wouldn't be fair. I may work with Rocky, but I have no idea how he thinks. It may surprise you, but sometimes I wonder if he's even thinking at all. Sorry, Ruby. I'm not your edge in this competition. Rocky doesn't tell me this kind of thing. Besides, he knows my own family will be hunting for it. There's no way he would share anything like that with me."

Ruby reached for a cookie, took a bite, and then smiled. "You misunderstand me, Betsy. I'm not asking you to tell me where the golden pecan might be. I'm asking you to give me insight into Rocky's habits. Where does he get his coffee, for instance?"

"Where we all do. We only have one coffee shop in town. Earl's."

Ruby bit her bottom lip causing just a tiny bit of lipstick to stain her teeth. "I suppose you're right about that. Okay. Where does he go after work? What does he do?"

"Well, okay. Some nights Rocky goes out to dinner with what he calls the widow of the week." Rocky was single, slightly handsome, and in his fifties, which made him quite the catch for the newly-unencumbered crowd. "But he's been trying to cut back on that. Said he's gaining too much weight."

"If you ask me," Maggie said, "I think some of these ladies are on to him. He's not coming over to their house to explore a new relationship. He's mostly coming over to dig into a new casserole."

"Okay. If not there, where does he go?"

"I don't know." I had never taken this much time to think about, much less talk about my boss. "He might spend time with his son. Sometimes he goes home. He might go over to one of the two bars in town—but he isn't much of a drinker. He's only there listening for any scoops on town news on a slow day."

"Not much there to work with. Who is his best friend?"

Everyone knew that my father and Rocky were close. They were often on either side of a criminal case, but it didn't matter. They had a shared history.

My aunt's brows furrowed. "Good grief, Ruby. It's like you never met the man. You've been living in the same city as Rocky for the last fifty years. Who do you think his best friend is?"

"Judd. I just thought he might have another. Maybe he's changing as he ages, branching out a little bit."

I shook my head. "And now you can see trying to get insight into Rocky's thinking is a waste of time."

Trying to get into a man's mind can be tough, especially if you fear he might never have had one to begin with.

Chapter 4

On the morning of the long-awaited treasure hunt, Pecan Bayou's finest and maybe-not-so-finest gathered at Benny's Barbecue to get ready for the opening ceremony. Birdie's Diner had a sign posted outside that read, CLOSED FOR THE TREASURE HUNT. Earl's Coffee had a temporary staff that was rumored to be taking forever, so the town descended on Benny and family. Town residents were enjoying a cup of coffee and one of Benny's wife's signature ginger muffins to start what would be an exciting day. Benny and Celia had four children, and it was a family affair as they attempted to wait on customers.

Because the hunt was such an exhausting endeavor, lasting twenty-four hours from 10 a.m. on Saturday to 10 a.m. Sunday, many people had decided to work in teams with an agreement that if one of the team members found it, they would take the cruise together or split up the cash reward.

Libby Loper, daughter of the late cowboy star, Charlie Loper, donated the prize, so she wasn't eligible to compete. Libby sat with Maggie and Ruby Green at one of Benny's tables. Ruby had convinced Maggie to go with her on the hunt on the condition that Maggie did not have to flirt with middle-aged Romeos. I was teamed up with Leo and the kids, one of many families competing to find the golden pecan.

Rocky was flitting about from table to table, trying to get a few short quotes from the contestants. He walked up to Ruby's table, pad in hand.

"So, do you think you're going to win the golden pecan, Ruby?" Rocky asked.

"I'm going to try," she said. She leaned forward just slightly. "Let me ask you something. Did you hide the pecan someplace similar to where you hid it last year?"

Rocky stopped scribbling on his pad and looked up over his reading glasses. "You know, I didn't go to one of those ivy league schools, but I don't think it would be very smart to hide it in the same place as last year."

Ruby batted her false eyelashes at him making me think of a scene in Bambi. "And just where was that? I can't recall."

"I can tell you that," Libby said, her turquoise bracelets dangling as she picked up a cup of coffee and took a quick sip. "He hid it over behind NUTV. Don't you remember that? It was in a cardboard box next to the dumpster. Very clever."

"Oh yes," Ruby nodded. "So, you're a hide-it-in-plain-sight kind of guy, then."

"Don't forget, I found it two years ago when the prize was a thousand dollars," Aunt Maggie said.

Ruby snapped her fingers. "Right. You did! It was in the pecan grove at the other end of Main Street. Hmm." She looked at Rocky again. "And it would appear you tend to hide things around established businesses in Pecan Bayou, right?"

"Why do I get the feeling that you're getting more information out of me than I am of you?" Rocky put his pad away. "That's for me to know and you to find out. The only hint I'll give is to follow the yellow tag. Or better yet—" He began to sing, "Spy a yellow ribbon on the old pecan tree."

Half an hour later, we were standing in the heat and blaring sun in Pecan Bayou's town square. Rocky stood with Vic Butler, and next to Vic was his beautiful wife Sarah, who was attempting to bring a cardboard box onto the raised platform. Everyone else had on practical clothing for what could be a dusty treasure hunt, but Sarah wore a clingy red dress and four-inch black heels. All she needed was a sparkling sash to complete the picture. The dress did little to conceal her ample cleavage, and she looked more like she was going out to dinner than to a treasure hunt. My stepson, Tyler, noticed her struggle and went to lift the box for her. Before he could get his hands on the box, he was bumped out of the way by Mark Valencia.

"Let me do it, kid. She needs a real man for the job." He flashed a smile at Sarah, who acknowledged him with a grin playing on the corners of her lips.

"Really, I'm fine," she said. "This young man—" Her gaze shifted to Tyler.

"Tyler."

"Yes. Tyler and I have it under control," she said, pulling away from the owner of Maximum Muscle.

"Come on, baby. I think you need a knight in shining armor right now, not a kid. I'm just the guy." It was obvious Mark wasn't used to taking no for an answer. Sarah and Mark could have been a perfect match, both being more attractive than the average person. She could have landed a job on the television show Baywatch in the '90s. I could see her bouncing down the beach in a red swimsuit, rescue board in hand. Mark was the six-pack-ab guy women imagined in romantic novels. They looked like the perfect trophy couple.

"You're sweet," she smiled.

Tyler blushed, placed the box on the stage, gave an awkward bow, and stepped back next to me. "She's beautiful," he said under his breath.

If there were such a thing as a pheromone catcher, I would have landed a netful. Tyler was smitten. To me, he was still a child, but according to the calendar, he was on the edge of adulthood, and today he was getting a good look at a real woman. Well, almost real.

My gaze drifted across the crowd. By my count, most of the town had shown up for the hunting of the golden pecan. This not being my first treasure hunt, I could easily classify the hunters into three groups. The first group was in it for fun and would last just a couple of hours. Then there were the more serious hunters like Maggie and Ruby, who would most likely make it for at least eight hours. Finally, there was the die-hard group that would power through until the golden pecan had been found. You could pick them out pretty easily because none of them were smiling. They reminded me more of Navy Seals going into combat rather than fun-loving Texans hunting for a goofy pecan.

Maggie and Ruby looked adorable, fanny packs attached, sun visors on, and each wearing a matching set of binoculars. Ruby had augmented her appearance with a bright orange vest so that Maggie would not lose track of her. It was an unusual wardrobe choice for her, but at least no hunters would be taking her down today.

"You sure are bright, Miss Ruby," Tyler said with a grin.

"Well, thank you. I wasn't sure if this matched my complexion, but I wanted to be especially visible when I give a hoot and holler after I find that golden pecan." You could find Ruby across Sleeping Beauty's overgrown forest with that vest.

Danny stood behind Aunt Maggie, his hand up over his eyebrows as he gazed at the sun.

"Morning, Danny," I said.

"Hey, Betsy," he answered. "It's too hot today."

"It sure is," Ruby said. "That's why your mama and I need to find the pecan fast."

"Good luck, ladies," I said before going to find the rest of my family.

"And good luck to you, baby girl." Maggie adjusted her visor and leaned closer. "I just know somebody in our family is going to get this cruise."

"You may as well go home right now," a low voice said from behind Aunt Maggie and Ruby. Earl Brown of Earl's Java stood behind them with another gentleman who looked vaguely familiar.

Earl stepped forward next to the man who had interrupted us. "I don't know if you ladies have met my brother. This is Bosco. He just got back from a, uh, long business trip and wanted to get here to hunt for the golden pecan."

"I didn't know you had a brother, Earl. Where have you been hiding him all these years?" Ruby asked.

Earl stuttered a bit. "Oh, he's been around. Mostly upstate."

"Yeah, I've been pretty tied up with business. You could say I couldn't get away." Earl's brother Bosco had on brand-new blue jeans, and I could still see the tell-tale threads on the back waist where a tag formerly resided. His crisp plaid shirt still had the folding lines of a newly purchased garment. On his head was a spotless Astros ball cap. He was not as heavy-set as Earl and had the build of a wrestler. When he smiled, he revealed the gap of a missing bicuspid. "Like I said, you may as well give up. If there's loot out there to find, I'm your man. I guess you could say I've made a career out of finding things."

Maggie tipped up her sun visor a bit to meet Bosco's eyes. "Let me tell you, Mr. Bosco. Don't underestimate two old ladies. We will most certainly find that golden pecan. We know this town backward and forward. You, my friend, are a visitor."

Bosco rumbled into a deep throaty laugh, making the sound echo over the sounds of the crowd milling around them. "So, you say, but my brother Earl has been living here serving you coffee all these years. If he doesn't know as much as you know, he's not as smart as I thought he was. Why don't you go on home and knit a potholder, little lady? That's more to your suiting. This right here is a man's game, and I could use that money from the cruise. I may go on a trip or I may buy myself a brand-new car. One of those sporty types. I need some wheels these days."

Earl stepped forward while at the same time putting an arm across his brother to pull him back. "You ladies are some of my most loyal customers. We wish you luck. My brother's just a little excited. May the best man or woman win."

Stan, the manager from NUTV and Howard Gunther, our local paranormal enthusiast, made their way through the crowd and took their place next to Ruby and Maggie. NUTV was the town's TV station bought for Stan by his parents twenty years ago. We always thought it was their way of keeping him in our tiny town and away from the bright lights of the city. He wanted to be in the entertainment industry, and what better way to do it than have a TV station? It was low-budget and featured shows like *Bowling with Beulah* and *The Farm Report*, but he was happy with it. Stan loved to wear bow ties, and today he had one on with matching yellow suspenders and navy chino pants.

"Hello, Maggie," Howard said. "I'd say we have a track record for finding things, being charter members of the Pecan Bayou Paranormal Society. Maybe we'll spot a ghost as a bonus."

"Good morning, ladies," Stan added. "Feels like a beautiful day. The last time we all worked together was the investigation of the old tuberculosis hospital. This should be fun." Howard gave Stan a grin and rubbed his palms together in anticipation. The two men made a strange, mismatched pair. Stan, dressed in his familiar bow tie, was as ever, incredibly neat. Howard Gunther looked a little like he had slept in his Hawaiian shirt and wrinkled khaki shorts. Stan would not only be participating in the contest but was carrying his camera and planned to do a few segments for the local cable access channel.

Birdie and a team of four waitresses all dressed in their customary blue Birdie's Diner uniforms stood with their arms entwined. "Did we miss anything?"

"Now, how are you going to make two tickets into four, Birdie?" Ruby asked.

"Not a problem. We decided to divide the cost of the cruise tickets and then pay the rest out of tips."

"Some of us decided that. I say we draw straws," Beulah Simpson said.

"You be quiet, Beulah. Let's give it to the waitress who has made the most in tips this year," Stacey Norman interrupted, her eyes glaring at Beulah.

"You be quiet. I've made more in tips than you."

"Have not."

"Have too."

Birdie might have a larger team, but whether or not they could agree on anything was going to be an issue.

"Yeah, and if you win, I'll have a big week at Earl's selling coffee," Earl smirked. "Once they've tasted my fine beverages, they may never come back."

"You might have the coffee, but we have the pie. They won't stay long," Birdie responded. There was a friendly rivalry between Birdie and Earl, especially after Earl decided to add breakfast burritos to his menu.

Mark Valencia walked to the center of the assembled group and held up his hands, hailing the attention of the crowd. "Hey, everybody. If you want to get into the best shape of your life, I have some coupons for the outstanding supplements at Maximum Muscle." He held up red rectangular pieces of paper splayed out like a poker hand, and several of Tyler and Zach's classmates from the high school walked over to grab them.

"Can I have a coupon for muscles?" Danny asked Maggie.

"You already have muscles. You don't need a coupon," Maggie answered quietly.

"It's trash," Bunny yelled out from the back of the crowd, raising a thin arm. "Don't put that poison in your body, boys. You're better off drinking herb tea than that commercially prepared God-knows-what powder."

"Not true," Mark yelled back. Tyler stepped over, and Mark handed him a coupon.

"This will bulk me up?" Tyler asked.

"You'll look like Arnold Schwarzenegger within the week," Mark promised. "Come by, and we'll discuss a supplement plan for you, kid." Mark continued to hand out coupons and ignored Bunny as she kept shouting about the evils of bodybuilding drink mixes.

Leo made his way through the crowd with Coco balancing on his shoulders, Zach trailing behind him. After a couple of hours, we decided the boys would take little Coco back to the house. I was surprised to see my father bringing up the rear of our brood.

"My, my, we have quite the gathering today, darlin'," he said.

Mayor Obermeyer called out from the stage, "Judd Kelsey, come up here. We need the law to start our festivities."

"Yes, we need you, Lieutenant Kelsey," Vic said as Sarah stood behind him. "We want to talk about appropriate behavior during the Golden Pecan Treasure Hunt." His wife smiled adoringly at him as he spoke. I loved my husband too, but it was rare you would see me showing such adoration in public. I glanced over to see Tyler's eyes glued to Sarah's every move as he held the Maximum Muscle coupon to his chest. Nothing like the hormones of a seventeen-year-old boy to make you believe in the power of lust. Behind him, I noticed Mark, now out of coupons, had his arms folded across his muscled chest. Even though he was years older than Tyler, he looked just as taken by Sarah's charms.

My father made haste to join the treasure hunt officials on stage. He turned to face the crowd, placed his hands on his gun belt, and got that long-arm-of-the-law look about him. The crowd started quieting down.

"If I could have your attention, please. Very good, very good," Mayor Obermeyer said. "Welcome to the annual hunt for the golden pecan. This year we're proud to have a wonderful seven-day cruise donated by Libby Loper, daughter of our hometown celebrity and famous cowboy star, Charlie Loper. Libby, would you like to say a few words?"

"Thank you so much, Mayor. Our prize cruise will leave out of the Port of Galveston and will take you to see the wonderful sights of Mexico and several Caribbean islands. What an adventure to exotic ports of call. And if you happen not to win, let me invite you to the Loper Dude Ranch, where you can play cowboy all day long. We have horseback riding, roping, a petting zoo, and our newest addition, the Charlie Loper theater, where my daddy is on the screen all day, every day."

The mayor took the microphone back before Libby could continue turning the opening speeches into an infomercial. "Thank you, Libby. We're so grateful for your generosity. And now Vic Butler, director of the chamber of commerce, will go over the rules and kick off our contest."

Vic reached back and squeezed Sarah's hand before he took his place behind the microphone. As he let go, I heard a loud *harrumph* in the crowd behind us. Turning around to locate the sound, I found Bunny scowling at Sarah. I'd never been a very good lip reader, but the word she was saying was plain to see. *Harlot*. Sarah took a step further back on the stage as if dodging Bunny's name-calling. What had Sarah ever done to Bunny? The women were exact opposites.

Sarah had done many things to improve her appearance which, from my observation, included plastic surgery, hair extensions, and fake eyelashes. She was not the little girl God had put on this earth, but a beautified version of herself. Bunny, on the other hand, did very little to augment her pale appearance. She wore a long stringy braid, large tortoiseshell glasses, a ruffled skirt that looked like it was fashioned from discarded pieces of a multicolored quilt, and Birkenstocks on her feet.

Vic continued, not acknowledging Bunny's attempted disruption. "So, these are the rules for the Pecan Bayou Golden Pecan Treasure Hunt. You will have twenty-four hours to find the golden pecan. Each team will receive a poem, and as you figure out one of the clues, it will lead you to the next location and another poem. We are observing a code of honor. If you find the golden pecan, it is your team's treasure only. If you run into a problem with an overzealous participant and feel threatened, similar to what happened last year, you can call 911, and—" He stopped and looked over at Judd. "Umm, Mrs. Thatcher, is competing with us. How do we handle that?"

Mrs. Thatcher raised her arm. "I'm not the only one in town who can answer the phone. We have Deputy Beckwith, who will be taking your calls day or night. We've stocked him with goodies from the vending machine, and we just have to hope there isn't a major crime spree during the hunt. I know no one will act up, isn't that right?"

Many people nodded their heads as if Mrs. Thatcher were their mother. Bosco did not nod. He looked bored, and I could tell he was going to be a problem.

Josiah Thatcher, a man in his sixties who wore red suspenders over his chambray blue work shirt, called up to the stage. "Let's get to the first clue." He turned to his wife. "The game's afoot, my love."

"We'll be drinking margaritas and relaxing on the boat in no time," Mrs. Thatcher replied, putting her arm around his waist. They had to be the cutest couple out here, and secretly I hoped they would win, even though Leo had some romantic ideas of his own.

"Arriba, Arriba," Josiah said.

"Arriba, Arriba," Birdie and the waitresses joined in.

"Shh," came from behind us. Bosco was glaring at our group. The more I was around this man, the less I liked him. Did he even have a right to be in the contest for the golden pecan? He didn't live here.

Earl elbowed him, but he ignored it. "I'd like to hear the directions if you don't mind."

"Sorry." Birdie looked back to me and lowered her voice. "Remind me to take that joker off my fresh slice of pie list."

Another "Shh" went up from behind us.

"All right, everybody. Settle down. Here is your first clue." Our attention was drawn to the front as Rocky pulled out a sheet of paper and began to read the official clue poem for the treasure hunt.

Today we are gathered to find the pecan
That glitters and shines.
Its lights are turned on,
You can search high and low;
Around the town, you will go.
Hear a moo and a sigh
At the beginning of your day,
Find the next clue, and you'll find
You're on your way.

I heard Earl whispering behind me. "See, I told you. The moo." Ruby heard it too, and turned around, facing Earl and his brother.

"You told him what? Earl, if I didn't know better, I'd say you already knew what was in the poem."

"Damn straight," Bosco responded before Earl could. "We know a lot of things, which is just another reason why you should give up. We've got the advantage."

"And how did you get that?" Aunt Maggie asked.

"Because Rocky had to channel his inner poet with a lot of caffeine. Where at? Earl's coffee shop." Earl had a glint in his eyes. "Rocky never got so many free refills that day."

Ruby gasped. "Do you mean to tell me you looked over his shoulder when he was writing the poem?"

"What's it to you?" Bosco smirked. "It's a free country, and the last I checked, it isn't a crime if I should accidentally look over somebody's shoulder when they are writing something. Not a crime."

"Except it's cheating," Aunt Maggie said.

"Yeah, you cheated," Danny repeated.

Sarah Butler began passing out a copy of the poem. The mayor took the microphone.

"And now without further ado...On your marks, get set...Go! And may the lucky nut win!"

Different groups started crowding around Sarah, anxious to get their copy of Rocky's poem. Leo grabbed my arm and pulled the kids and me into a family huddle. "All right, team, this is how we work. First of all, any ideas as to the meaning of the poem?"

Zach held up our family's copy. "We know it has to do with cows, so I say we spread out and check the fields within the city limits."

"I don't think we need to go too far on that one," I said. "There is only one field to speak of. There is that land next to Dilly Dairy Ice Cream where they graze cows every once in a while to get the agricultural exemption for taxes."

"Yes, are there cows there now?" Leo asked.

"I don't think so, but we can drive by."

Maggie came up to the group, Ruby and Danny behind her. "We're off in search of a cow. Ruby thinks it might apply to the cowskin purses in the store window at the Charlie Loper Gift Shop." Libby had recently opened the store to sell cheap cowboy trinkets and encourage people to drive out to the dude ranch.

With the clue being so vague, it could be anything even remotely related to a cow. As we drove over to the field, there were no cows grazing at present. Leo pulled over. "Well, that's not it. Where else?"

"Maybe we should go look at cowskin purses?" Tyler asked, barely looking up from his phone. I glanced over as he scrolled through pictures of weightlifters. Tyler was an athlete and participated in football, basketball, and baseball. He didn't need to add more muscles, but it was clear he was being lured in by Maximum Muscle and the prospect of looking like the men in the pictures.

"Sure," Leo said as he made a U-turn to return to the town. When we got there, we found Maggie and Ruby inside the Loper gift shop.

"Any luck?" I asked when we joined them.

"Nope. Ruby, though, saw something she had to have, so here we are, wasting time," Maggie said.

"Hush, Maggie. Those boots are on sale," Ruby said in a sing-song voice, reflecting the true happiness of spontaneous shopping. "Have a heart. Besides that, you bought a little notebook."

Maggie held up a notebook with a picture of Charlie Loper on a horse, a still shot from one of his countless old films. "I bought the notebook so I could keep track of all the details." She turned to me with one of those looks where she was about to tell me something wise. "We not only have to keep track of what we do but what everyone else does."

When we exited, Coco pulled on my arm. "I have to go tee tee." Her big brown eyes shone up at me.

Tyler stepped up. "Yeah, I think I've already had enough of this wild goose chase. I'll take her home."

Zach's phone buzzed. "Me too." He had been spending a lot of time texting someone at school. The way he was being so secretive about it, my bets were on a girl.

"But we just started. I thought you wanted to do this." I couldn't believe my kids were pulling out of the fun in the first hour of the treasure hunt.

"Right, so we can win you a trip and get to babysit Coco while you're cruising," Zach said.

Leo put his arm around my shoulder. "Fine. We'll get more done without you sad sacks anyway."

Coco put out her bottom lip. "I'm not a sad sack. I'm a happy sack, and I still have to go tee tee."

Leo picked her up. "You're a happy sack. Mommy and Daddy will take you back home. Make sure Tyler and Zach take care of you."

Unsure if the boys could handle a precocious preschooler, I left a list of instructions for them to follow to make sure Coco was watched and fed on time. I only hoped they took the time to read them.

Chapter 5

I tried not to feel too guilty about the relief that crept in as we said our goodbyes to the kids. After all, treasure hunting with an almost five-year-old could only lead to tears once the boredom set in.

As Leo parked the car in one of the diagonal slots in downtown Pecan Bayou, I held up the clue. "I have an idea about the *moo* mentioned in the poem."

Leo turned the key and shut off the car. "Let me guess, it's the mooooving company down the road?"

Now that we were kid-free, Leo and I relaxed. This was turning into a great day to spend together. "Very funny. No, I think it is the Cattleman's Call."

Pecan Bayou's one steakhouse had a large plastic longhorn steer out front. If you squinted almost to the point of closing your eyes, it actually looked real. "You just might be on to something, Watson," Leo said in a strange British accent with a decidedly Texan edge.

I unbuckled my seat belt and looked over at Leo. "Why do I have to be Watson? I came up with the idea."

"Ah yes, Betsy, the happy clue hunter." He used the same accent, making me want to cancel my cable access to the BBC.

"Thank you." I pulled myself out of the car. We were parked in front of Maximum Muscle, where a crowd of boys came out of the shop with bags full of supplements. Those coupons must have paid off for Mark. The downtown shops were surrounded by a series of alleys that served as a conduit for trash pickup. That way, the trash truck didn't cause any Pecan Bayou traffic jams. With only one traffic light in town, it didn't take much to cause a traffic jam. "If we cut down the alley, we can probably get there quicker."

Leo gave me a bow and a flourish and continued to speak in faux Brit. "Lead on, m'lady."

As we turned the corner into the area behind the store, Bunny Donaldson stood with her hand in a trash can positioned next to Maximum Muscle's alley entrance. There were boxes neatly stacked by the can ready for pickup. Mark Valencia obviously took pride in being tidy. The alley itself was free of stray trash and had been swept clean.

"Will you just look at this poison?" As she emphasized the word "poison," her braid dipped to one side. "The men in these pictures don't look healthy. This is not what a real man looks like. These guys are pumped full of steroids. He should be arrested for distributing this trash. People in this city need to know that Mark Valencia is nothing more than a steroid peddler."

Bunny began to throw brown glass vitamin bottles against the wall, her mood spiraling out of control.

I stepped forward, trying to grab her arm. "Bunny. Stop. You're getting glass everywhere."

"So what? It's no worse than the mess the devil in that store is creating. At least you can sweep up my mess. You can't sweep up the effects of toxic chemicals rotting away your insides. He's peddling substances that will ruin those kids' livers, turn them violent, make them bald as a billiard ball."

"I know this is upsetting for you, but these are vitamins, not steroids. You don't have any proof for your claims." I grabbed at a small glass container in her hand.

Bunny wrenched her arm away. "Then I'll get proof. What if he's providing steroids to all those boys? You just wait and see. I'll prove it."

Leo nodded. "Then prove it, but for right now, you need to stop throwing glass bottles around."

"Fine. I'll go directly to the problem then."

She pushed past us and headed for the front of the store. As we watched her go, I whispered, "She's going to get herself into trouble with her temper. I also don't think it's a good idea to confront the store owner with nothing to back up her accusations."

Leo sighed and pushed aside a piece of broken glass with the toe of his sneaker. "Bunny doesn't have that kind of self-control." Taking me by the elbow, he guided me through the broken glass. "Let's keep moving."

"It sounds like you want this seven-day cruise as much as I do."

He smiled and raised his eyebrows. "Hmm, seven days all alone with my wife. How will we fill the time?"

"I'm sure we can think of something to do," I grinned.

When we came out the other end of the alley, I spotted a big yellow envelope resting on an artist's easel next to the cow in front of Cattleman's Call.

"There it is!" We broke into a run to get to the envelope. At the same time, the Thatchers crossed from the other side of the street. I made it to the easel first and pulled out a sheet of paper.

As Mr. Thatcher pulled out their copy, I began to read out loud:

You found clue one

But you're not done.
The robins sing,
On Charlie Loper take wing.
My gaze met Leo's. "This is terrible poetry."

Josiah muttered, "What the hell does Charlie Loper have to do with anything?"

"What do you think, Mrs. Thatcher?" I asked.

"Listen, Betsy. I know you've called me Mrs. Thatcher since you were a little bit of a girl, but with us doing this hunt together, I feel like you should call me by my first name."

All these years, I had never known her first name. To me, she was always Mrs. Thatcher, the dispatcher. "What *is* your first name?"

"Primrose."

"Really?"

"You can call me Prim."

"Okay, Prim. What do you think?"

Prim tapped her chin. "The robins sing. Maybe the next clue is at the pet store? Minnie has a few birds in there."

"I guess." Josiah did not sound particularly sold on the idea. He turned to me. "What do you think?"

I shrugged. "Maybe?" Secretly I was harboring the theory that the poem was describing birds that loved to land on the statue of Charlie Loper.

"We're heading to the pet shop," Prim said as another group came down the street. Aunt Maggie, Ruby, and Danny were in the rear.

"There it is!" someone shouted, and a thunder of footsteps started toward us like it was a Black Friday sale with free TVs.

Maggie and Ruby started running toward us, veering off from the crowd.

Leo tugged at my elbow. "We don't have time to help them right now. This is our chance to take the lead," he said. "Have to go, Aunt Maggie. No time to talk." He steered me back to the alley. "We'll get there sooner if we take our shortcut."

"Do you think it's in the park by the statue of Charlie Loper, too?" I asked, hoping that was the direction we were headed in. Charlie's statue used to hold a six-shooter until someone knocked it off, leaving his impolite middle finger greeting visitors to Pecan Bayou. The town council had to have a sculptor come in and reshape the hand to look like some sort of halfhearted wave, as if he were saying, "Welcome to Pecan Bayou...maybe."

"Has to be," Leo said.

"But we were just there. How could we have missed the clue?"

We stepped back through the broken glass. The back door of Maximum Muscle was now open, but a stillness had settled in the alley. Bunny must have finished telling Mark off for selling what she thought was poison. Maybe she ran to find a policeman to arrest him? The buildings that surrounded the alley left it in shadows, and after being in the bright sunlight, it took a little for our eyes to adjust. Leo, who was ahead of me, tripped and fell into the broken glass. He made a groaning sound followed by a thud as he hit the ground.

I stopped, letting my eyes adjust to the shadows before I made the same mistake.

"Leo, are you all right?"

"Yeah. I'm—" He stopped mid-sentence and jumped up. "Oh, my God. Call 911. The muscle guy. He's—call 911!"

I punched in the numbers and drew closer to the prone form of Mark Valencia and tried my best to describe what I saw to Deputy Beckwith.

"Is he alive?" I could hear the crinkle of cellophane on the other end, so Deputy Beckwith was clearly enjoying the snacks Prim had left for him.

"I don't know. He's lost a lot of blood." My eyes had adjusted to the dimness of the alley, and I bent over to try and locate the source of the bleeding. There was a gash at his throat, and what looked to be the jagged edge of one of the brown supplement bottles I had seen Bunny throwing around earlier appeared to be embedded in his neck. The sickeningly sweet strawberry odor from the liquid vitamin permeated every inch of the alley. It was a sickening mix of fruity scent, vitamins, and blood.

"Check the store," I said to Leo as I held the phone. "Bunny was just with him. Make sure she's all right."

"You say Bunny was with the victim? Is she still there?" Beckwith asked.

"We're checking."

"I have an ambulance on the way."

Leo bounded in through the back door. "Bunny?" he called out. "Are you in here?"

I picked up Mark's wrist and checked his pulse but couldn't feel anything. His eyes were closed, and his head listed to the left. Deep red blood puddled on one side of the body, and I took note of where my feet were and stepped carefully back to avoid getting blood on my canvas shoes, or contaminating the crime scene. Someone had slit his throat and left him to die in the alley. From the amount of blood on the pavement, and the location of the cut, it had to have been his carotid artery. With that deep of a cut, death wouldn't take long.

Leo was breathless as he returned to the alley. "Bunny isn't in the store. We can only hope she got away from whoever did this."

"Are you okay, darlin'?" My father ran into the alley behind me. He was followed closely by his partner, Lieutenant Boyle, our big-city transplant. Boyle immediately approached the body.

"I'm fine. We were running down the alley and Leo tripped over...Mark."

Dad tipped his Stetson back. "Is that the muscle store guy?"

"Yes."

"What's sticking out of his neck?"

"Glass," Boyle said as he leaned closer.

I nodded. "I think it's from one of the broken bottles of liquid vitamins he sells."

My father surveyed the area, now small particles of glass glistening where the sun was cutting in through the open back door of the shop. "How did all these bottles get broken?"

Leo shook his head, his elbows at right angles against the doorframe. "Bunny Donaldson. When we came through here earlier, she was shouting the evils of his products and broke a bunch of empty glass bottles."

"It really was a shame because Mark kept a tidy alley," I added.

My father made a face I had seen many times. He was zoning in on a crime scene. It was like he was seeing the act of murder replayed in his mind—or at least that was what he told me it was like. "Uh huh."

Orley Ortiz, one of two ambulance drivers employed by the city, parked at the end of the alley, and began to unload his gurney. My dad raised a hand. "No need to hurry. Mr. Valencia has passed."

Spotting me, Orley said, "Hey, Betsy." He turned back to my dad and gave him a knowing smile. "With your daughter on the scene, I guess I should have known." He flashed me a look, humor in his dark brown eyes. I was so happy my bad luck in finding bodies had become a running gag at the fire station.

On the park side of the alley, a crowd had begun to gather, and at the front, Sarah Butler looked pale as Vic held her. Belinda Donaldson, ticket book in hand, stretched her neck out slightly to get a better view.

"What happened?" Vic asked. "And what's that smell?"

"Wild strawberry liquid vitamins. Someone slit Mark Valencia's throat," I informed him. Sarah placed her hand over her mouth and looked away.

Ruby stepped in from behind Vic, lifting her visor as she took in the scene only a few feet away. "Good Lord, what's that sticking out of his neck?"

"Glass. He was murdered," Sarah whispered. "There's only one person around here who would do a thing like that. Where's Bunny Donaldson? She hated Mark almost as much as she hates me."

"Now, don't go blaming people. It's way too early for speculation," Dad said.

Belinda stepped closer to Sarah and glared at her. "He's right. My sister wouldn't do that. You need to think twice about making accusations in front of the whole town."

"That woman has killed him. I tell you, it was her," Sarah said, her tone now more emphatic.

"Shh," Vic whispered in Sarah's ear as if she were a small child. "We should go and let the police do their jobs."

My father turned toward the crowd. "Did anybody see anything?"

His glance immediately shifted to me. "We didn't see anything, but Bunny Donaldson was back here having a temper tantrum throwing bottles around and threatening to tell off Mark."

"Yes. She was accusing Mark of selling steroids. When we left her, she was going into the shop to have it out with him," Leo added.

My dad scratched at his ear and thought for a moment. "With all due respect, Belinda, your sister Bunny is as crazy as a loon, but I don't think she would actually kill somebody." He began to mumble to himself. "The craziness that comes with this hunt gets worse every year." He turned back to the crowd. "I'll be sure and question her, though."

"I should think so," Sarah said.

Vic Butler questioned, "Does anybody know where Bunny is? Has anyone seen her? Belinda?"

"I have no idea where she is," Belinda answered.

"The last contact we had with Bunny was when we heard her in the shop," I said. "After we found Mark's body, Leo went into the shop to see if Bunny was in there. He was afraid the killer might have gone after her, but there was no sign of her."

My dad directed Boyle, "Go by Bunny's house and see if she's home."

"I'll go with you," Belinda said.

"You're going to Bunny's house?" Rocky asked as he bit his lower lip.

My dad cast a look of frustration toward the town's newspaper editor. "That's what I said, didn't I? You have a problem with that?"

"No," Rocky answered. "Just asking as a member of the press."

Prim stepped forward. "Judd, do you need me back on the switchboard?"

"Well, I can't deny it would be a comfort to have you there, but you deserve a chance at the golden pecan just as much as everyone else."

"You know I put the safety of this town before anything. I'll just check in on Beckwith and see if he needs any help. If he does, I can send Mr. Thatcher on the hunt by himself. It only takes one person to find the golden pecan."

My father nodded. "Thanks, Mrs. Thatcher."

"Do you need me, Dad?" I asked.

"You can probably move on, but before you do, can you tell me the exact time that you saw Bunny going off to confront Mark?"

I looked at Leo. "I would say it was about forty-five minutes ago."

Dad studied his watch. "That would be at 1:15 p.m."

"Yes."

"Hmm. He's a pretty big guy, and she's little, and that would give her about twenty minutes to commit the murder and skedaddle out of here without anyone noticing. A woman taking down a man can take double the time of a man-to-man fight. From what I can tell, he was stabbed here in the alley, possibly in the doorway. The blood spatter tells me he died here."

I looked around. The neatly stacked boxes were now scattered across the alley, and there was one smaller box that had been ripped open and discarded. Even though Bunny had been throwing bottles, I didn't see her throwing down an empty box like that and then just leaving it behind.

"Does this mean the hunt for the golden pecan is canceled? Damn." Surprisingly, Ruby still stood in the alley. Maggie wasn't there, and neither was Danny. I guessed Maggie must have taken Danny elsewhere so he wouldn't see the body.

Rocky stepped closer and took a quick picture and then turned to the gathered citizens. "No. The hunt is not off. Please feel free to mill about all the top-notch businesses in the downtown area, but the alley is now officially off-limits. There wasn't anything here anyway."

Even though Leo and I had started our journey down the alley running, we now walked out to the park to find the next clue box.

Aunt Maggie joined us when we re-entered the street. "Where is Danny?" I asked.

"The minute we heard something was going on down here, we sent him to the library with his chapter book. He has his phone with him and has been told to stay there. Cora Jean, the librarian, is watching over him."

"I'm glad to hear you have it covered. Danny couldn't take seeing this."

"You're telling me," Maggie said, catching up to me.

"Don't suppose you saw which way Rocky went?" Ruby asked.

"I heard him say he was going to try and hang around Bunny's house if Boyle found her. I think, now that he has a picture, he might try to run back to the Gazette office to get the story into the computer."

"Then I'll just peek over his shoulder." She turned to Maggie. "Come on, Maggie. The hunt is back on."

"If you say so," Maggie answered.

They took off in the other direction, and as soon as they were out of sight, Leo and I ran to a small yellow flag at the back of the gazebo. Because Libby had funded the restoration of the structure, it was now called the Charlie Loper Gazebo. That was how it tied into the clue. The old-fashioned, white raised octagonal stage was used by the local volunteer band in the summer, where they would play strains of anything from "Achy Breaky Heart" to "The Orange Blossom Special." At Christmas time, Santa held court each Saturday in December. As we ran to the box, I noticed Stan and Howard. They had caught sight of our haste and began to follow us. Stan was a cross-country runner and quickly outpaced Leo and me.

"It's over here, Howard!" Stan grabbed a yellow envelope, and Leo grabbed ours.

Howard, who was many years older than all of us, ran up, hands on his knees, panting. "Good job, Stan."

"I had a feeling there was something here." I knew that Howard was referring to a sixth sense or extrasensory perception (ESP), neither of which he had.

"It's easier than that. When Betsy and Leo go running across a field, there must be something there." Stan grabbed his camera from his bag and began to film Leo as he held up the poem.

"Read it for us, Leo," Stan said. "You're used to reading off a script."

Even though Leo did do a short stint as a weatherman at NUTV, he still was not all that comfortable on camera. His eyes searched out mine, and I nodded as if to say *go ahead, you can do this*.

Leo began to read.

You're getting closer,
Yes, you are.
This calls for a drink
At a favorite Pecan Bayou bar.

Chapter 6

Howard cocked his head to the side. "Hmmm, a bar. Well, that narrows it down to the only two within the city limits. Which one?"

I pointed in the direction of the closest bar. "We'll take Goin' Nuts, and you guys take Bubba's Beer."

"Maybe we should take Goin' Nuts," Howard said, raising his slightly sunburned nose in the air. "How can we be sure you don't know something we don't, working with Rocky and all?"

"Okay," I sighed. "We'll take Bubba's." It didn't matter to me.

Howard put a hand to his chin. "And how do I know that maybe you didn't trick me into going there all along? The old reverse psychology ploy."

Stan grabbed Howard's arm. "Enough, Dr. Deduction. We'll take Bubba's."

As they walked off, Howard said, "Good call. I knew she was up to something."

"Good luck," I called out.

We walked toward Goin' Nuts, the bar named after Pecan Bayou's only cash crop. Leo opened the door for me, but I backed up.

"Let's look around the outside of the bar first. Maybe there's a clue in an empty box like last year."

After circling the building to look for any visible golden clue boxes, Leo shook his head. "I don't see anything, do you?"

"Nope."

We stepped inside the murky pub lit only by neon Lone Star beer signs. The refreshing burst of air conditioning tempered the smell of stale beer that hit me when we entered. We found Salty Collins cleaning off the bar.

"What can I get you?" Salty asked.

Leo stepped forward. "Uh, we're looking for the golden pecan."

Salty scowled. "Are you now? We have plenty of gold here, but it's liquid—on tap."

I straightened a bowl of nuts that was precariously situated on the edge of the bar. "Sorry. I just wanted to straighten that out. It only takes a minute to make your business look appealing. So, you're saying there are no clue boxes hidden here?"

Salty held up both hands. "Do you see any clue boxes?"

"Not immediately." We did a visual scan of the entire bar. When we were satisfied there was nothing there, Leo and I started for the door.

"I told you," Salty called after us. "Next time, order a beer and don't waste my time."

"I'll bet Howard and Stan found it," I said. As the sunlight hit our eyes, the Thatchers came running across the parking lot.

Mrs. Thatcher extended a hand and waved a finger at us. "See, I told you. Betsy and Leo are there already."

Josiah stopped to catch his breath. "Calm yourself. We'll find it."

I realized Leo was still holding the yellow envelope from the last clue, and there was a chance the Thatchers thought we'd found a new clue at the bar. Now I found myself in a moral dilemma. I had known Prim since I was a small child and had memories of her giving me lemon drops from her desk drawer. She had been nothing but kind to me, but was this the time to tell her the truth or simply let her believe the wrong information?

Not my finest hour.

As we ran away from Goin' Nuts and headed toward Bubba's, we crossed paths with Ruby and Aunt Maggie, and not wanting to stop, gave them a quick wave. Ruby stepped forward, ending the friendly exchange. "You have another clue. You're ahead of us. You should share it."

"Fair is fair, Ruby," Leo said. "You've got to find the clues on your own. Just go back through the first clue and figure it out."

Ruby scowled. "So, that's how it's going to be. Every man and woman for themselves. Fine, but when I'm drinking those Mai Tais watching the moonlight on the sea, you can bet I won't be thinking of you."

"I find great comfort in that," Leo said grabbed my hand and steered us away. "Come on Betsy, let's keep moving."

It did seem unfair not to help them just a little bit. "I'll give you a hint. Turn around and go back the direction you came." Ruby looked back at the park.

"You mean Rocky would do something as lame as hiding a clue in the middle of the park? The central meeting place of the town? I swear this contest is for amateurs."

They ran off in the other direction while Leo and I made our way back to the second bar. This establishment catered more to millennials, so it was generally cleaner and less creepy, but still no clue box. When we came out, Stan and Howard were sitting at an outdoor table with two tall glasses of lemonade in front of them.

"No luck," Stan muttered. "I thought for sure it would be here. It's getting too hot to search. The temperature is close to 100."

"Are there any other bars around here?" I was beginning to feel tired from running and sat down at the table next to them.

Howard snapped his fingers—he'd had a revelation. "They sell liquor in the grocery store!"

"Could be," Stan took a drink of his lemonade. The conversation stalled, and then after gulping down the remainder of their drinks, the other team took off without a word.

"Yeah, I don't think it's the grocery store either," Leo said as he took a seat next to me. He pulled out the clue. "Go to the bar and have a drink. The only problem is we're fresh out of bars."

"What other kind of bar is there?"

"Candy bar?"

That was a good idea, but in this heat, setting up a clue that wouldn't melt would be difficult. "I have no idea." Leo's stomach grumbled. "I could use a little lunch. Maybe filling our stomach will help to fill our heads."

When we got to Benny's Barbecue, I pulled out my phone to text the boys. I needed to make sure they would remember to get Coco some lunch. Deciding this was something close to a date, Leo and I went all-out and ordered milkshakes. Leo's head was bent over the yellow clue paper as he tried to figure out what the poem really meant. As the restaurant started filling up, it was obvious we weren't the only ones who were stuck. A couple of booths over the Thatchers were digging into salads. Vic and Sarah Butler sat down at the table next to our booth. Sarah still looked in shock, and Vic got up to use the men's room. I looked over and smiled at her.

"Are you doing okay?"

She grabbed her napkin and dabbed at the back of her neck. "Not really. Has your father arrested Bunny for the murder yet? I'll be glad to get that woman off the street. It could be me next, you know."

Her soft dulcet tones reminded me of Marilyn Monroe. She gave a little squeak and took a bite of her sandwich.

"Do you really think Bunny is capable of such a thing? She makes no bones about her complaints, but she seems harmless to me."

Sarah looked up, blue eyeliner encircling her eyes. "Not to me. It's just there's been so much death in Pecan Bayou lately, what with Poppy going over the bridge and all."

Benny came over with our waters and then rushed off to take care of another customer. Leo took a sip and then asked Sarah, "Can I ask why you and Bunny don't get along?"

"I'm not exactly sure. She's made some pretty wild claims about me. Not just the way I dress and look. She thinks I'm fake, but I think she blames me for something more."

Leo set his glass down. "What?"

"I don't want to go into it right now. But once Bunny gets onto something, she can't let go. Look at poor Mark. She decided he was poisoning people with the fitness products he sold. I just can't believe he was doing anything illegal. Although I heard he was doing some pretty fast business."

"With whom?" Leo asked.

She gave a pouty smirk. "I'm really not sure. Some sort of shady types, Vic said."

Now this was interesting, I thought. "Do you know who any of those shady suppliers were? It might give the police a starting point in their investigation."

She took in a breath, making her ample bosom rise. "I know he had a meeting with that Bosco guy." She glanced around the room. "I don't trust that guy as far as you can throw him."

I remembered the large man from the opening ceremonies of the golden pecan hunt. I didn't realize he was in the muscle-building business, but he certainly had the physique for it. "You mean Earl's brother?"

"That's the dude. He was so rough looking you would almost think he was a criminal or something."

Vic returned to the table. "Are you ready, my dear?"

"Sure." Sarah grabbed her purse and looked back at us. "Thanks for the talk. Not everyone in this town takes the time to be nice if you know what I mean."

"We need to talk to Bosco," I told Leo, once the Butlers were out the door.

"No. We need to tell the *police* to talk to Bosco. We're trying to win a contest, not solve a murder." Leo reminded me.

"Fine," I said as Celia came out of the kitchen, balancing our milkshakes on a tray. Just as she started to turn, another diner bumped into her and our drinks tumbled, splashing the sweet milky drink against a poster of this year's football schedule. Football is a big deal in Texas, so the Friday night lights crowd would be expecting a clean schedule post haste. My father always said that if a young man can throw a football endless distances and can think under pressure, he can achieve anything.

"Benny just put that schedule up," Leo said as chocolate shake dripped over the center bar of the uprights. "Tyler was checking it last week to see when the first game was."

The bar. "That's it. I've got it. I know what the bar means."

Leo's eyes widened. "What?"

"We have to go."

"But our food. They're remaking our shakes—" he protested.

"Make it a to-go order, and we'll pick it up in twenty minutes."

After getting Celia's promise to hold the food, we ran to LBJ High, Pecan Bayou's only high school, named after Lyndon Baines Johnson. Even though it was a hive of activity during the school year, right now it was peaceful. The football stadium was behind the school and surrounded by fencing with no gates. The principal said the configuration was for security, so they could keep track of people attending sporting events, but I think it was because it routed everyone by the snack bar and souvenir table. I sprinted across the field to the far goal post. There was an envelope on the center bar of the goal post but much too high for either of us to reach.

"What will we do?" I asked.

Leo looked up at the yellow envelope. Judging by the pristine state of the clue box, it didn't look like anyone else had been here. "Get up on my shoulders," he said.

"Are you sure? I do weigh a few more pounds than Coco." Our daughter loved to ride around on his shoulders, and as much as I loved watching it, I never considered doing it myself.

"Just do it."

Clumsily I climbed up on his shoulders as if we were about to play chicken in the pool. I heard him groan at my added weight. Once we seemed stable enough, I reached up to the waiting packet of clues. My hands barely reached it at full stretch. When I extended my legs to grasp the paper, Leo lost his hold. We warbled like a too-tall stack of LEGOs and collapsed onto the grass.

"Oooh, that's going to hurt tomorrow," Leo said.

"Maybe so," I said, rolling over. "But we'll be busy..." I pulled out the clue. "...planning our seven-day cruise!"

He grabbed the clue, laughed, and kissed me. "Oh yeah, baby."

"Well, ain't this sweet? Rollin' around on the ground with a clue." Bosco stood above us, his beefy arms crossed. Earl stood next to him, his focus on the goal post.

"How did you get up there?" Earl asked.

I gathered myself and rose from the deep grass of the football field. Knocking the dirt off with my hands, I answered, "It wasn't easy."

Bosco put a hand to his chin as he considered the solution. "I get it. Only way you could have reached it was on his shoulders." He locked his hands together as if offering to help me mount a horse. "What do you say, little lady? Care to help out a couple of nice guys?"

He seriously wanted my help? I stared at his hands.

"Come on, I don't bite. Well, not unless you ask me to." He raised an eyebrow, and now my skin was crawling. No wonder Sarah didn't like the guy.

"You're on your own, guys. We have to head out." Leo pulled me toward him.

"One more thing," I said to Bosco. "I heard you knew Mark Valencia. But I thought you were new to town."

Bosco's features hardened. "What's it to you?"

"I was just curious."

"Well, curiosity can be dangerous." His gaze slid to the clue box. "Tell you what. Climb up and get that clue for me, and I'll spill my guts. How does that sound?"

"Betsy." There was a warning tone in Leo's voice.

"I'd be glad to help...if you'll talk to me." I walked back over, put my foot into Bosco's extended hands, and he boosted me up to the goal post. Once I grabbed the clue, he brought me down with his hands on my waist. We were so close I could smell the coconut mocha coffee on his breath.

"We have to keep meeting like this," he whispered and then gave a low chuckle.

"Not if I can help it," Leo pulled me away.

Bosco started opening the clue.

"Wait," I said. "A deal's a deal. I want to know how you know Mark Valencia."

Bosco didn't even look up. "I sold him some stuff I picked up in Houston."

"What kind of stuff?"

"Well, duh. What do you think? Stuff to make those high school boys get big muscles."

"That's it? Just run-of-the-mill nutritional supplements?"

"Yeah," his lips began to move as he read the clue to himself, Earl reading over his shoulder.

"Nothing illegal?"

He stopped suddenly. "What are you saying exactly? You accusing me of something?"

"Uh, nothing," Leo said. "We'll be going."

We ran to the back of the bleachers, and Leo ripped open our clue.

There were three sisters
In Summer would wallow.
Two in front
The little one followed.
If you can find the key,
You might find yourself on the sea.

"This must be the last clue," I said.

"Whose family has three sisters?" Leo asked.

"Bunny Donaldson."

Chapter 7

Bunny Donaldson lived with her sister Belinda in a quiet, two-story brick home with a big front porch. Some of the paint on the window frames had blistered in the Texas heat over the years and the roof needed repairing. The Donaldson women were the only set of three sisters we knew in Pecan Bayou, and this was where the two surviving sisters lived. We saw no sign of a clue box but we did see Bunny's car in the driveway. She was at home. We tapped on the dilapidated screen door. The solid door was open, and inside a soft whirr of new-age flute music played.

"What do you want?" Bunny asked, speaking through the mesh of the screen, her nose nearly touching the door.

I didn't know quite where to start, so I tried being civil. "Hi, Bunny."

"What do you want?" she repeated slowly, as if trying to speak to someone in a different language.

"Uh, right. We think you might be connected to a clue in the treasure hunt."

Leo stepped up. "You are one of three sisters."

"Two sisters," she corrected. "Poppy's dead."

"Yes, we heard. We're so sorry for your loss."

Bunny continued on, almost as if we weren't there. "I should have known the way she flitted from job to job that she wasn't long for this life. Belinda hasn't stopped knitting since it happened. It's her form of therapy. We're a house in mourning. Go away."

"But you are the only set of three sisters in town."

"So?" Bunny started to close the door.

I gave her my most convincing smile. "Could we look around your house for just a minute?"

"You mean, come inside?"

"This is the house you grew up in, right?" I asked.

"Listen to me. I've just gotten back from the police station, and I have a terrible headache. You think some half-assed clue led you to my house? I don't give a damn about that ridiculous nut, or this contest, so go away."

"You were questioned about Mark's murder?" I asked. I was surprised she was let go already with so much evidence pointing directly to her.

"What do you think?"

I suddenly felt guilty for what had to be a very uncomfortable interview with the police. They wouldn't have questioned her if I hadn't steered them in that direction. "I guess we should tell you that we told the police about you throwing bottles and your plans to confront Mark."

She shook her head and squinted her eyes. "Should have known it would be you. But what about it? I had every right to confront him. He was selling poison. What's worse, he was selling it to *children*. He had to be stopped."

I dipped my chin down and asked, "By stopped, are you saying—"

"I killed him? Of course not! I'm a pacifist. Just count the number of cats running around this place. I don't believe in killing anything—even something as undeserving as Mark Valencia, the poison peddler."

"You have to admit it looked pretty bad. You were the last person to argue with him before he was murdered. It also doesn't look good that he was murdered with his own products—the ones you were seen throwing around."

"I know exactly how it looks. I threw a few of those so-called vitamin bottles around, but only a few were made of glass. Most of them were plastic, just like the everything else in this over-packaged nation. Don't they know plastic will be here longer than the sun?"

"Did you know anything about other substances being sold there?" I asked.

"Like what?"

"Steroids?"

"Of course. Everyone in town knew. He was a scavenger on the bones of our youth. Besides that, when he was being given his just reward, I was back at my store, restocking the hummus. It sells out very quickly."

"Were there any customers there who can vouch for you?" I asked.

"Excuse me, why would I need to justify my whereabouts to you? You're not a cop. Frankly, I think you're as annoying as your father. Go on and get back to your treasure hunting."

Even with the shade of the front porch, the heat surrounded us like an overstuffed quilt. The voices of other treasure hunters were growing closer. "We were just trying to help. I would think you'd want to clear your name," Leo said.

"If I want your help, I'll ask for it. I'm an innocent woman, and that's all I need to clear my name."

Even though it had nothing to do with Mark's death, I asked one more question. "Why do you hate Sarah Butler so much?"

Bunny's lips drew together in a thin line. "Seriously? Can't you see she's just as plastic as those little bottles of poison? She's not a real woman. She's a Barbie doll."

"You hate her because she's had breast implants?"

"Breast, jawline, booty. I bet if you pushed her in a pool, she'd bounce like a beachball. What would possess a woman to fill her body with so many artificial substances? I haven't had any work done, and I have the same figure I had when I was eighteen."

Bunny clearly wasn't going to confide in us, and it was likely we would need her cooperation in the future, so I tried to smooth things over. "You're a testament to healthy living. Listen, sorry we had to tell the police about your argument with Mark."

Bunny smirked. "Do me a favor?"

"Yes?"

"Stay out of my business from now on. I don't need any more favors from the likes of you." She slammed the door in our faces.

Well great. Bunny could be sitting on the final link to the golden pecan and not even know it. Even though I had told Ruby I had no idea how Rocky thought, I realized crafting part of the puzzle around a person no one liked would be just his idea of fun. I knocked on the screen door.

She yanked it open and glared. "What?"

"Read this." I thrust the paper in front of her face.

"It's a clue in the hunt for the golden pecan," Leo said. "You're the only one we know with two sisters."

As Bunny began to read, her mouth dropped.

"Are you telling me that every yeehaw in Pecan Bayou is going to come running to my house looking for that stupid pecan?" She walked toward the back of her house and returned shortly with an ancient-looking shotgun. I could see rust on the trigger. If she shot that thing, there was a chance it might backfire on her. "There is no clue to that toxic nut at the Donaldson residence. You hear?"

We backed off the porch, taking careful steps not to trigger anything. "We hear," I said, my hand in front of me as if I could stop a bullet.

"There will be others," Leo said.

"And I have the same exact answer for them. Bang. Bang."

As we left Bunny's house, Leo's phone beeped.

"It's work. I'll be right back." He walked off with the phone to his ear. Leo was a meteorologist, and this time of year, we were deep into hurricane season. It was like being married to an obstetrician nine months after a full moon.

"Betsy!" Maggie came power-walking across the park, Ruby behind her with a more stylized walk. "I need to ask a favor."

"Okay," I answered, noticing how flushed her face was. I knew I was hot, but how was the heat treating my elderly aunt? Maybe she really didn't want to go on that cruise after all.

"It's Danny. Do you think we could get the boys to watch him too?"

"Sure. Is he still at the library?"

"Yes. I'm just afraid of what he might be hearing over there. People do talk, especially when it involves murder. Ruby and I can pick him up and drop him at your house."

"No problem."

"Thank goodness for your boys. They're so responsible."

I *almost* agreed with her. There were days when they were anything *but* responsible. But this year, with the help of Marie Kondo, I had tidied up that area of my life as well. There would be no "I'm bored" coming out of the mouths of my children. I created summer schedules—laminated and hung prominently in the kitchen—to keep the kids on task. This would not be a summer wasted on hanging out. I had both boys' summer reading lists posted, as well as little nudges to review their math skills during the summer. Take a minute to do a little something, and it can change your life. Kids today don't have enough self-discipline, and I was doing my best to combat the pull of phones and computers. All a part of the Marie Kondo method.

"How are you doing on the clues?" I asked.

"Not good," Ruby said. "How about you?"

"We're stuck."

Leo walked over to us, holding his phone out slightly. "I need to deal with this."

"Sure, that's fine. I need to help Aunt Maggie get Danny situated at our house anyway. I can also check on our *responsible* babysitters."

Leo gave a curious smile as he walked toward the car with his phone. Could it be he didn't quite trust my description of our sons?

When I walked into the house, Coco was in the living room by herself, painting flowers on paper plates. And furniture. And walls. And the carpet. Butch trotted out of the kitchen at the sound of my voice and his tail, wagging away, was now a bright purple.

"Where are the boys?" I asked Coco.

"Tyler went to some lady's house, and Zach is upstairs on his 'puter.'" I picked up the paint pots before she could do any more damage.

"You go to the bathroom and start washing up in the sink. I'll be there in a few minutes. Clean up Butch's tail too. That can't be good for his skin. I'm going to have a talk with your brother."

Her smile deflated. "Don't you like my flowers?"

"I like the ones you painted on the paper plates. All the rest I don't like. You know better than to paint on the walls. And the dog."

Coco stuck out her lower lip. "You don't like my flowers."

"I do, but— Oh, just go wash up." Coco launched into a wail that could challenge a fire siren. Zach came bounding out of his room.

"Coco?" He spotted me on the stairs. "Oh. Hi Mom. Back already?"

He sounded so casual as if his sister hadn't personally redecorated the den with primary colors.

"Where's your brother?"

"He went out. Some lady called him and said he could make some cash."

"Who?"

He put both hands up in the air and shrugged. "How should I know. He told me to watch Coco, and he would be back."

I pulled him gently down the stairs. "And this is how you watch her?"

"Oh, my God." As he took in the damage, he began to laugh. "Oh, God."

"Coco is not the only one to blame here. Being in your room with the door shut is not watching her. I hold you both responsible."

Zach's eyes widened. "What? I was upstairs reading a book. A book from my reading list. I thought you'd be happy. What about Tyler? He completely split. Doesn't he get some of the blame too? That isn't fair."

"Oh, Tyler is in a whole other batch of trouble. Don't you worry about that. Go get the paper towels and the household cleaner and start washing down the walls. I'll put Coco in the tub."

Zach began plodding toward the kitchen, mumbling, his hands in his pockets. "Really? I have to do all the work while Tyler's out with the hottest woman in town?"

I was halfway to the bathroom when I stopped short. "Excuse me? I thought you said you didn't know who called him."

"Uh, did I? My bad. It was Mrs. Butler. You know, Miss Sarah." Zach couldn't hide the little smile on his face. He might have been angry with his brother for leaving, but there was also admiration in his eyes.

"Why did she want Tyler?"

Once again, the shrug. "Who knows? Maybe she thinks he's sexy."

I pulled out my cell phone. Tyler was about to be a senior in high school and had grown into a handsome young man, but he was still under eighteen. Sarah Butler might be flirting with him, but I'd be damned if she was going to try to seduce my son.

"Tyler?" I said when he answered. "Where are you?"

"Uh..."

"Are you with Mrs. Butler?"

"Yeah." He seemed surprised I already knew. "How did you know that?"

"Zach told me. Why did you leave Coco alone?"

"I didn't. Zach was watching her. It doesn't take two people to watch Coco."

"When you see what she did to the den, you may change your mind. You need to come home right now."

"Can't. I'm...uh...helping Mrs. Butler replace water bottles at the rest stations for the treasure hunt. I can't leave until I finish the job."

"Where is Mrs. Butler?"

"Right here. Did you want to talk to her?"

"Uh, no. Just finish the job and come directly home, do you understand me?"

"I'm not deaf, Betsy. I get it."

When I hung up, I found Coco creating a mountain of colorful bubbles with the soap in the sink—bubbles that were floating and landing all over the bathroom counter and floor. I quickly got her into the tub.

"Are you mad at me, Mommy?"

"Some, but I am also very disappointed in your brothers."

"Don't be mad."

When she looked up at me with those repentant brown eyes, it was hard to stay mad for long.

"I'll work on it."

When it comes to parenting, carrying a grudge doesn't help anything. Actually, that could be said for life in general. I wondered if Bunny Donaldson's parents ever told their three little girls that? My mind drifted to Tyler as I scrubbed paint off Coco. He should have been home reading a book, getting ready for the next school year. Didn't he realize how much was at stake this year? He needed good grades to get scholarship money. He could be in control of his own destiny if he'd just put in the work.

After grabbing dry shorts and a t-shirt from Coco's beautifully organized drawers, I returned to the bathroom and pulled Coco out of the bath and dried her off.

"Betsy, we're here," my aunt's voice echoed from the front door.

"Hey Betsy," Danny said.

"Danny's here!" Coco started wiggling as I quickly dressed her and then made a quick escape and ran to her cousin to hug him. I picked up the wet towels in the bathroom and then joined the assembled group at the bottom of the stairs.

"Danny! Will you teach me how to ride my bike without training wheels?" Coco asked. Leo and I had both promised to help her make this big step but hadn't followed through. I had more time than Leo, but every time I thought of letting go of that bike seat, I found myself stalling. Was she ready for this yet? She could crash and hurt herself. It would be my fault for pushing her into something she wasn't prepared for.

"Oh, I don't ride my bike that good, Coco," Danny confessed.

"You don't have to ride it, just stand behind me and hold onto the seat."

Maggie cut in. "I don't think that's a good idea. Danny gets distracted sometimes and might forget to keep you steady."

Coco heaved a gigantic sigh and slapped her hands on her knees. "Okay." She dragged out the word like she'd been denied an organ transplant.

"We could play a game," Danny said.

"Or," I said, "Coco could take a nap. Will you help Zach keep an eye on her?"

"Sure," Danny said. He beamed, proud to take on the responsibility.

After all the commotion, it didn't take much for me to convince Coco to lie down for a nap. Maggie left to join Ruby, and Tyler came tromping in after his impromptu job for Sarah Butler.

"Tyler, in here," I said from the office.

He came up the stairs, and when he stood in the doorway, I could tell from his expression I had cramped his style.

His shoulders were rigid, and from the color in his face, I could tell he was angry. "Really? I've been trying to find work all summer, and when someone finally calls me for a job, you tell me to get home?"

"Yes, but you promised you would look after your sister. You could have at least called your father or me and told us what you were doing."

"I left Zach here to watch her. I can't help it that he didn't do his job. You can't blame me for this."

On the one hand, he was right. He had thought to leave his brother in charge before dashing out the door to help a damsel in distress. "Fine," I said. "Why did Mrs. Butler call *you*? She hardly even knows you."

"Uh, I don't know."

"Uh-huh." Considering he had just spent an hour out in the heat, Tyler didn't even look sweaty. I still had my worried that the woman didn't even think of asking for his help until she saw Tyler flex his muscles at the opening of the Golden Pecan Treasure Hunt. Why was Tyler so evasive about what he was doing with Sarah Butler?

"Were you really only carrying around cases of water?"

"Yeah. Sure. Well, we talked a little too. She's really upset about the Maximum Muscle guy. I can't believe you and Dad found him."

"Was she friends with him?"

"I don't think so."

My cell rang on the desk. Tyler took that as his opportunity to run off.

"Hey, Bets. I'm done," Leo said. "Can you meet me in the town square?"

"Sure." We were back on the trail of the golden pecan and the three sisters. Not sure if it was a good idea, but I left Coco, the mistress of abstract painting, in the hands of three babysitters and wondered if they would be enough.

Chapter 8

One thing good about a small town is that the town square is nearby, no matter where you are. As I walked over, I noticed several of the contestants still wandering around with yellow clue sheets in their hands. From what I could tell, Leo and I had gained some time by figuring out the goal post clue, but Stan and Howard had been there too. How far along were they by now? Maybe they had already found the golden pecan and were inside somewhere enjoying the air conditioning.

I was anxious about telling Leo what had happened with Tyler and his impromptu job. I felt sure nothing had happened, but it was just strange that she would call Tyler when she had a perfectly capable husband who could have done the job. I could guess why she would want Tyler to do it. He had grown into a handsome young man who, based on physical appearance, could go on a television dating show and win it all. But his maturity level was typical for his age, and he was definitely not ready for a Mrs. Robinson affair.

As I strolled past the Pecan Bayou bank, Vic Butler came out, holding his cell phone. I debated telling him about his wife summoning my son and decided discretion was probably the better path at this point. Then my mothering instinct took over, and the discretion thing was shot.

"Say, Vic. Can I talk to you about something?"

He looked up, surprised at my presence, and then pocketed his phone. "Sure. Is it something about the treasure hunt?"

"Sort of. It's about water bottles."

"Water bottles?" He tilted his head forward.

"Yes. Sarah called my son, Tyler to help her replenish the stock at the various rest stations."

"She did?"

"Yes. Tyler said it was a last-minute thing."

He let out a sigh and as the sun hit his face, he looked much older than usual. "I see. I find this very interesting. You say she called your son?"

"He's about to be a senior in high school. He was the tall kid who offered to help your wife lift that box this morning."

"Oh, yes, of course. She probably got a bit overwhelmed trying to keep up. I had to tend to some business and left her on her own, poor thing. Thank your son for us, will you?"

"Sure. He was happy to do it. I think he might have a little crush on your wife."

Vic placed his hands in his pocket, his gaze drifting down the street. "She's a stunning woman. Who could blame him?"

Could being married to the most beautiful woman in Pecan Bayou be a bit of a trial for the bank president? It was proof positive of the old saying, *Be careful what you ask for*. Vic Butler clearly had more than he could deal with.

"And I am the parent of a teenager who doesn't always know the right path to choose."

"Okay, I'm going to say something that that may be hard for you to understand. There are a lot of things going on with my wife, to say the least. Sarah sometimes feels like she doesn't have any friends."

"That may be so, but a seventeen-year-old boy would not be an appropriate friend."

"No, you're absolutely right. But Sarah is a lost soul. Something in your son must have appealed to her."

"He's a senior in high school, for goodness sake. If she is looking to become his friend, I don't think that would be good for him. Like you said, she's stunning. Tyler is a young man. Let's do all we can to nip this blossoming friendship in the bud."

He paled and then gulped. "You've made that very clear." He took me by the arm and pulled me out of earshot of passersby. It was then I noticed a tear in his eye.

"I'm so sorry," he said. "Sarah's lonely."

"That's a lot to have to deal with. Thank you for letting me know what's going on. It helps. I hope you get a handle on it."

"For our marriage's sake, I hope so too. I still love her, even after all she's done. I'm just worried someday she'll get herself in a situation she can't get out of. She had recently befriended another gentleman in town. Of course, now—"

"Are you talking about Mark Valencia?"

His face paled. "I don't want to talk about it." Vic turned and walked away, his shoulders slumped.

After I left Vic, Leo was waiting for me in the town square. "You made it!" he said, kissing me. "I was beginning to think you'd given up treasure hunting for an afternoon nap."

"Nope, but I do have a few things to tell you about."

"Uh oh. I never like the sound of that."

I quickly filled him in on Sarah and Tyler. Leo bristled. "Seriously? He's just a kid."

"Who looks like a man. The person I feel the worst for is Vic. He wants to help his wife but doesn't know what to do."

"I suppose you're right. I just have a tough time believing all of this. You know, as a father, you think you are going to encounter this sort of thing with your daughters, not your sons."

"It's a new day, Leo. Boys can be as vulnerable as girls," I said, linking my arm in his. "And now, Mr. Meteorologist, what's going on with the weather?"

"Oh, around here, it's clear, but elsewhere there are some storms coming up. The urgent call had to do with software problems." Leo rolled his eyes.

"And you're the guy they call, right?"

Now that the sun was really beating down, there were almost no treasure hunters on the street, most of them having given up or sitting somewhere cool trying to figure out whatever clue they might be stuck on. Not yet acclimated to the heat, I suggested we visit the library.

"Funny time to want to check out a book," Leo said.

"Yes, but the perfect time to see if there are any other families with three sisters. They have the census records over there. There are also the fifty years of newspapers we can search through."

"Fifty years? We'll be there for the rest of the day."

"Come on. You're the guy whose head is in the clouds all the time looking for anomalies. You can handle it."

When we entered the library, Maggie and Ruby were sitting at a table writing out notes.

"Well, here you are," Maggie said. "We were beginning to think you gave up, darlin'."

"Not quite. How are you doing?"

"We're still struggling. We've been to every bar in town..."

Ruby smiled, looking a little uneven. "The best part of the treasure hunt so far."

"Ruby had a few beers seeing as both establishments said treasure hunters had to purchase something," Maggie said. "But we still can't figure out the clue. How about you? Did you find it?"

Leo nudged me. "Um, can't say."

Ruby's nose went up. "Okay. So that's the way we're playing it."

"Ruby, don't say it like that," I said.

"You're in the library with us." Ruby tapped my shoulder. "So that means wherever you are in the treasure hunt, you're stuck too. Right?"

"Maybe," I scowled. Earl came out of one of the stacks holding a book about guns of the world just as Bosco entered from the street.

"How you doin', brother?" Earl asked.

Bosco strode across the library, his long legs taking it in just a few steps. "How do I look like I'm doing?"

"Like your same old rascally self. Why is it we've been separated for years, but you never stopped being my big brother?"

He gave Earl a backhanded head bop. "Are you done looking at city maps? I've never found anything useful in a place like this. I'm all about hands-on. Why read about it when you can do it?" His gaze drifted toward me. "We meet again. I have to tell you I really enjoyed our little hug."

Maggie and Ruby's heads turned to me in whiplash fashion.

"Have you been questioned by the police yet for your business dealings with Mark Valencia?" I asked. "Is that where you've been?" Just how hands-on had he been with the supplement store owner?

I felt Leo's hand on my arm. "Forgive my wife. She's the daughter of the investigating officer, and sometimes she can't help herself. When you grow up with a detective, you tend to think like one."

Earl shrugged. Bosco gave me a sour look. I guess his memory of our little hug had just faded. "Whatever," Bosco said. "I think you'll find it's better for your health if you keep it to yourself, lady. You get my message?"

His message was loud and clear. "But you told us you sold him things for his business. I should think any contacts with Mark would be a part of the investigation. Did he make you angry about something? Was he trying to cheat you?"

This time Bosco's look hardened. "Who the hell are you?" He turned to his brother. "You never told me this town is full of soccer mom busybodies, Earl," he said and then turned directly to me. "Mind your own business."

"Well? Did you sell him steroids?"

"Betsy," Leo whispered.

"And if I did, what of it? I suppose now you're going to question anyone who ever set foot in that guy's store? Ask me one more question..." Bosco clinched his fist and started to raise it.

I felt Maggie behind me. "Or you'll *what*? Punch my niece out in the public library? Not while I have a breath in my body."

"Or me," Ruby said.

"Shut the hell up," Bosco exploded, causing the librarian to issue a "*Shhh*."

"Let's go, Bosco." Earl started pushing him to the door.

"Yeah, don't want to be around these yocals anyway. I'm going to win your prize, suckers. You may as well go home," Bosco said as he passed through the glass doors.

"Betsy? What was that all about?" Leo asked.

"I don't know. There's just something not right about that guy."

"Good old Betsy. She might look like a mild-mannered housewife and helpful hints columnist, but deep down inside, she has the soul of a G-Man," Ruby said.

All these compliments had me feeling pretty good. No one had ever said I had a soul of a G-Man before.

Maggie pointed a finger at me. "So, do you think that Bosco the bully did it?"

Leo stepped up. "She doesn't have time to speculate. We're here to do some research for the clue that we're on."

"And what clue would that be?" Ruby could be persistent and wasn't planning on giving up anytime soon.

Leo smiled. "Why don't you work on your clue, and we'll work on ours?"

Chapter 9

Once we were out of earshot of Ruby and Maggie, Leo let out a sigh as we walked along Main Street. "Now that the Donaldson sisters are out of the picture, I've been racking my brain trying to figure out where we go next."

I stopped walking. "I think we should go to Maximum Muscle."

Leo nodded automatically, but then as my words sank in, he stopped. "Why would we want to go there?"

"Because we need to know more about what Mark was doing before he was murdered. Was it a deal gone bad? Was Mark trying to cheat Bosco, or was it the other way around? If we look close enough, will we find a motive for murder?"

I was almost sure that whatever was going on there with the investigation, I could get into the store. After all, technically, the crime scene was in the alley.

Leo ran a hand through his hair in exasperation. "Betsy! We're in the middle of a treasure hunt. You are not a police detective. Did you forget that fact? We're running out of time. How do we know there aren't other teams ahead of us? Think about it, sweetie. Seven days. On the sea. You and me... alone. Please tell me it hasn't been so long that you've forgotten what it's like to be alone, free from the constant flow of interruptions from three kids?"

I put my hand on his cheek and gently pulled him closer. "I know. Think about the three *sisters* and no, I haven't forgotten what it's like to be alone without teen hormones and preschool capers."

Leo drew closer, taking me into his arms. Seven days just might be exactly what we both needed.

"What's that you're saying about three sisters?" The Thatchers had come up behind us, Josiah's cheeks flushed against his white hair. "We've been searching for hours and can't figure out what this means. Did you come up with a new idea?"

"Not yet."

"I take it you've been to Bunny Donaldson's house?" Prim asked.

"Yes. I think we were the first to visit her."

Josiah gave a *harrumph* and then did a once-over on Leo and me. "And from the absence of bullet holes, I guess you came away unscathed."

Prim shook her head in disgust. "If I had a nickel for every time that nut job has called the police, I'd be a rich woman today and have no need to be out here in the heat, competing in a treasure hunt."

"Yes," Josiah said, "the missus here comes home all the time talking about that crazy woman. Rocky should have thought about the fact that the clue would lead us all to her house. I'm sure the police report will be the most interesting thing to read in the paper tomorrow. Bunny has always been a little crazy, but since the death of her sister, it's grown worse."

Could it be that Prim knew something about Poppy Donaldson's death that I didn't? Whenever I would ask my father, he remained stoic. "I never did quite understand what happened to her. Something about getting attacked that night when she was out fishing?"

"That's what I heard too. Strangest thing ever. They found her the next morning in the water under the Pecan Bayou bridge. From what they could tell, she fell from the bridge, hit her head on a rock and landed face down in the water, poor thing. She drowned."

"What was she doing out fishing in the middle of the night?"

"Let's just say she and Bunny were not all that different." Prim fanned herself with a folded clue sheet. "The Donaldsons have been night fishing for years. Strange for most people, but not for the Donaldsons. My guess is they don't enjoy fishing next to the fine citizens of Pecan Bayou. Belinda, the oldest sister, is the only one that turned out right. She doesn't seem to have the demons that Bunny and Poppy had. Maybe it's because her name doesn't end in a *y*. Why do women always have to have those cutesy names that end with the 'e' sound? Bunny, Poppy?"

Leo cleared his throat. "And then there's my lovely wife, Betseeeee."

"Oh, sorry," Prim said. "Well anyway, Belinda is the best knitter there is around these parts. Showed me a cable stitch I've been trying to do for years."

Josiah took off his glasses and cleaned them with the edge of his shirt. "Yeah, well, Poppy's death sounds fishy to me, pardon the pun. I fished for years off that bridge and have never even come close to falling off."

"Did Poppy have a history of any kind of drug abuse or a problem with alcohol?" I asked.

"I heard Poppy made her own beer in the garage, but I never heard anything about her being drunk or anything. Of course, with Bunny in the house, it was probably all natural. Organic. Fit in with their back-to-nature way of thinking," Josiah said.

"You're right. It is fishy. Bunny's sister died by falling off a bridge that nobody falls off of."

No wonder Bunny was so angry at the world. She'd had a sister who shared her house and her interests, and without her, Bunny had become an angry old woman.

Leo stepped in. "But we are still all stuck at the same clue—the three sisters."

"Yes, we are, and it doesn't help we're trying to work around the crime scene at Maximum Muscle. You can bet there's stuff going on that we're missing," Prim said. "I'm used to being at the pulse of this town. This is one of those days I wish I was at work so I could keep up with the investigation on the police radio."

"Did you know much about Mr. Valencia?" I asked. I hadn't thought of Prim as a resource before, but the only difference between her and Ruby was that she was exposed to the heart of the town gossip, but unlike Ruby chose not to talk about it to every cut and curl that came in the door.

Her eyes darted from side to side, as if searching the street to be sure no one caught her in the act of leaking information she normally kept to herself. She absentmindedly pushed up the glasses on her nose, and I noticed the heat and humidity had taken a toll on her beehive hairdo. Tiny tendrils of frizz were poking out around her head. "Let's just say that some of Mark's activities were being closely monitored by our local police."

I waited for her to say more, but she stopped. There was a reason why my father liked working with her, and this was one of them. Rocky had been trying to get information out of her for years, but she could keep a secret quite well. Her loyalty to the department was legendary. Maybe it was the heat, or because I was Judd's daughter, but Primrose Thatcher was ready to talk.

Not wanting to give her time to change her mind, I asked, "What kind of activities?"

She waved her hand at me as if to assume a nonchalant air. "Oh, you know. Muscle stuff."

I wondered if she had heard anything about Mark selling something that was not legal. "I heard he was investing in steroids," I said. "I also think that Bosco Brown might have been the person who was selling it to him. What do you know about Bosco?"

"I can tell you about old Bosco," Josiah spoke up. "Went upstate to prison about ten years ago. Heard it was car theft of some type. Earl was talking about it one day in the coffee shop. You know they're not from around here. Earl said when they were kids, Bosco was always in trouble. When Bosco went to prison, Earl decided to relocate and start a life for himself here in Pecan Bayou. Sometimes the best way to get away from temptation is to start your life somewhere the devil hasn't found yet, and that's what I think Earl did. Too bad that no matter how far you run, your relatives can find you."

"I hate to interrupt this discussion of our town's unsavory characters, but let's talk about three sisters," Leo said, his frustration building.

"Let's," Prim echoed.

Now that we were getting back on track, Leo smiled. "We can definitely say it's not Bunny and her sisters, so who could it be?"

Josiah nodded. "I've lived in this town for sixty-five years, and the Donaldsons are the only family I can think of that had three girls. Could it be we're supposed to go out of town?"

"No," Leo said, "All of the clues have to be reachable on foot within the city limits. That's the rule."

We stood in silence for a moment as the sun burned down the back of my neck. I wished I had some of Aunt Maggie's aloe plant juice to put on it. Ruby had sworn by it for years. Ruby. Maggie. "I know this sounds crazy, but could it be three women who are not related? Women who think of themselves as sisters?"

Prim tapped her chin. "Now, that is an interesting idea. Where do we know three women who are close as sisters?"

The idea was becoming clearer to me, but I wasn't sure if I wanted to share it with the Thatchers. I suppose we could outrun them in a foot race, but the question was whether we would choose the correct location first. Three sisters. Why hadn't I thought of it before? What three women in this town were like sisters? Maggie, Ruby, and Libby Loper. But whose house would the clue be at? Libby's ranch was considered out-of-town, but she used to live in a house at the edge of the park. As far as I knew, she still owned the property. It could also be at Ruby's salon, The Best Little Hair House in Texas. As far as Maggie's house, I think she would have found Rocky snooping around her yard, trying to put up a yellow clue box. Besides that, the last time there was somebody snooping around her yard in the middle of the night, she shot at them.

Rocky would think twice before rustling the bushes outside of her house without telling her first. In my moment of sorting out possible locations, I had grown quiet and had not noticed the rest of the group staring at me.

"You figured something out, didn't you?" Leo asked, rubbing his hands together in anticipation.

"Maybe, but I'm not sure. Leo, let's go."

"Fine," Prim said. "We'll give you a ten-minute head start, but if we pick up your trail after that, it can't be helped."

Leo tipped his baseball cap. "Good enough. Thanks, Prim."

"You won't be thanking me in a little while when we get to that prize before you. We might be old, but we're speedier than we look and have experience and wisdom to throw into the race."

Once we got away from the Thatchers, I explained my theory to Leo about three sisters being Maggie Ruby and Libby. Leo nodded.

"So that means we need to check all three of their places," I said.

"The Best Little Hairhouse is on the way, so let's go there first," Leo said.

"But it'll be closed. She closed it for the treasure hunt."

"That doesn't mean they clue might not be outside somewhere. After that, we'll go to Maggie's house."

"Are you kidding me? The last time anybody crept around Maggie's house—"

"I know, the Christmas creeper."

I thought of when Maggie shot who she thought was the Christmas creeper. Someone had been peeking into ladies' windows at night, and Maggie, deciding not to be a victim, shot out in the dark. That was a decision she came to regret.

"Don't worry. After visiting Bunny, I think I've got the duck-and-dodge move down." Leo moved like facing off Olympian dodgeball athletes.

Chapter 10

As we made our way to the town square and Main Street, I glanced over at the Pecan Bayou bridge and thought of Poppy Donaldson's suspicious death. The metal bridge crossed the bayou, separating our downtown area from the school complex, which contained our elementary, junior high, and high school buildings as well as the football field where we had found our last clue. The bridge, built almost 100 years ago, had metal slats on the top and concrete on the bottom. The metal had turned to rust in many places, making it look more red than gray. The distance to the water was enough to throw out a line to fish and a person would probably break a bone if they decided to jump. I never thought it would kill a person. But freaky accidents happen all the time, right? I visualized Poppy Donaldson going off the bridge. Did she really hit her head, or did someone else cause her death? Maybe the reason Bunny was so angry all the time was because she thought her sister had been murdered. Even so, you would think she would be spending more time harassing my father and the Pecan Bayou Police Department and not Sarah Butler.

Perhaps if I discussed Sarah's recruitment of my teenage son with Bunny, I would find out what the bad blood was between the two women. As we turned the corner onto Main Street, Vic drew closer and gave us a handout.

"It's a scorcher today, so we just wanted to let you know that we have set up refreshments in the high school gym along with various stops around town. We wouldn't want anybody to be suffering from heatstroke. We still have a few more hours of the high sun, so please be safe."

The sun was beating down on us. There was nothing like the angry heat of a summer Texas day.

"Betsy mentioned that Sarah asked Tyler for some help," Leo said.

Vic drew closer. "We are so grateful for his help and for the kindness your family has shown. She told me you had a nice conversation at Benny's. Sarah's always had problems making friends when she's not in a beauty pageant, and this treasure hunt has been difficult for her."

This was confusing to me. You would think anyone who was as pretty as she was would find making friends easy. "Why would this be difficult for her?"

"Social anxiety, you know, and she also suffers from somnambulism and night terrors."

"Wow," I said. "I had no idea she had all that going on."

"Yes, it's been very difficult. And, well, in light of the day's stress, I decided that Sarah should go back on her medication even though it sedates her. I'm afraid it's rather heavy, but because of the night terrors, I'm hoping it will help her sort out things in the end. This murder of Mark Valencia really upset her, as it would anyone. What a gruesome death."

"I'm sorry to hear that," Leo said. "But it sounds like you're on top of the problem."

The smile returned to Vic Butler's face. "When it comes to Sarah, I try hard to do the right things. She is precious to me. Whoever would have thought a woman that beautiful would be interested in a man like me." He stopped, maybe feeling he had said too much and took up a more businesslike tone. "Thank you so much, and please stay hydrated."

As he walked away, Leo said, "Well, I guess that's that. A beautiful woman has to be sedated in order to control herself. That seems strange to me."

"And night terrors. He didn't mention that part before."

When we walked up to The Best Little Hairhouse in Texas, the door was firmly locked and the shades were drawn. We made a trek around the entire building, including the alley, but found that there were no clue boxes. I was beginning to think that my three-sisters theory was wrong.

I grabbed Leo's hand. "Let's go to Libby's. We can't go outside of the city limits, but we can hit the gift shop."

Libby was behind the counter when we entered, restocking a lovely assortment of turquoise earrings. The minute she spotted me, she held up a pair. "These would look good on you, Betsy. Of course, everything looks good on you."

The store was empty except for us. Rocky's plan to raise sales in the downtown area did not seem to be working for Libby.

"We were wondering if we could check your store for a clue box," I said.

Libby looked confused for a moment. "My store? You can certainly look around and even purchase a few things, but Rocky wouldn't have a clue here. I'm too much a part of the contest. It wouldn't look good if someone I knew, which is everybody, came up with the golden pecan because of me. That goes for my house in town as well."

I sighed. "I guess you're right. We have a clue about three sisters and thought maybe the sisterhood of you, Maggie, and Ruby might be what the clue refers to."

Libby closed the glass case behind the counter. "Well, isn't that nice. You know I never had any sisters, being an only child and all. I think having Maggie and Ruby as sisters would be right lovely."

When we reached Maggie's house, instead of finding a clue box, we found Danny sitting on the front porch, his elbows on his knees.

"What are you doing out here, Danny?" I asked. The last I had heard Danny was looking after Coco. Did Maggie know he was here sitting on the front porch?

"I got tired of watching Coco sleep, and I know my way home. It is five blocks. I count them as I go. One. Two. Three. Four. Five. Do you have a key to my house?"

Aunt Maggie would be livid when she found out what Danny had just done. I scrambled in my purse for an extra key Maggie had given me years ago. "Did you tell your mom you were leaving our house?"

"No." He looked down at his red, scuffed, Converse All-Star sneakers. "Mama is going to be mad, but I just wanted to go home, and she is so busy with the big gold nut. Miss Ruby says they are going on a trip on the ocean. If she goes on a trip, I will be here at the house alone. I've been in the house all by myself before, but sometimes I get scared. I thought if I went home, I could get used to it. For the big trip on the boat."

He stood as I unlocked the door. "Will you tell Mama? Am I in trouble? I was being the man of the house."

I put my hand on his shoulder. "Yes, I will tell your mother, but I'll also tell her why you did it. I think she'll be upset about it at first, but in the end, she'll understand. You need to know that if your mom is not around that we'll take care of you. Do you understand that? You won't have to be in your house alone. You're a part of our family, as well as your mom's."

"Yes, Betsy, but I miss my mom when she goes away."

"Well, who knows. She may not find the golden pecan. Lots of people are looking for it, even me and Leo."

Danny smiled. "Yes. You could go on the trip. That would be good, and then Mama would stay here with me."

"It could happen, and if I have anything to do with it, it will," Leo said with a sparkle in his eye.

"I think this will go over better with your mom if we just take you back to our house. That way, she won't be angry with you. Is that okay?"

"I guess so. Can I wake up Coco, so we can play?"

"No," Leo and I chorused.

Before we could walk the five blocks home, Prim and her husband drove up and parked in Aunt Maggie's driveway.

"Thank goodness we found you. Judd asked me to find you. Your Aunt Maggie has been attacked. She's in the hospital. It seems Ruby was off talking to somebody, and when she found Maggie, she was knocked over, and the notebook she was keeping was gone."

"Mama?"

I wished Prim had thought about Danny before blurting out her news. I took hold of his hand. "I'll go check on her, and I'll let you know."

"I want to go with you."

"Just let me check on her first, okay?"

"Okay."

Leo gently touched my cheek. "I'll stay here with Danny. You go to your aunt." I scrambled to the Thatcher's car, and Josiah hit the gas. This couldn't be happening.

Chapter 11

When I got to the hospital, I began preparing myself for the worst. I imagined my aunt in the ICU awaiting brain surgery. Did they even have a brain surgeon in a town as small as Pecan Bayou? Instead of a room full of monitors and stone-faced nurses, I found her in the triage section of the emergency room sitting at the end of a hospital bed. Her feet dangled over the edge, and she was holding an ice pack to her head. The expression on her face was more impatience than clinging to the mortal coil. She gave me a grateful smile as I entered through the curtain that separated her from the other emergency room occupants.

"Come to spring me out of here?" She clutched her pocketbook to her chest with her free hand.

"Only if the doctor says you're well enough to go. I'm so glad you're all right. Prim scared me to death. She said you had been attacked."

"I don't know what happened. There was a scuffle, and I fell and hit my head. I think it was an accident, but I'm not sure. Bosco was involved, but it was all so quick. That's all I can remember right now. My little notebook is gone, did you hear that?"

"Yes, but if that's the worst of the damage, it doesn't matter. I'm just glad you're okay. When things like this start happening, it makes me question whether this yearly hunt is such a good idea. I mean, look, it has attracted someone like Bosco Brown."

"Ruby went to confront Bosco, but if I know her, there might be some shopping on the way. I need to get up and check on Danny. I've been calling him every hour. I don't know why I bothered to buy that boy a cell phone when half the time he doesn't have it charged, or for some reason, he doesn't bother to answer it. Where are my shoes?"

"This probably won't make you feel any better, but Danny got tired of babysitting Coco and decided to make his way back home."

"Land sakes. Was he okay?"

"Leo's with him right now."

"Thank God you two found him."

"He was sitting on the front steps. We had this crazy idea that one of the clues might be at your house."

"My house? You're right, that is crazy. What made you think that?"

Once again, I had said too much. If I explained our reasoning, she would find out about the three-sisters clue. "That's a story for another time. I was just so worried when I heard about you. You're not as young as you used to be. Are you going to press charges?"

"I hadn't thought about it. I'm still unsure whether I was attacked or not, but right now all I want to do is find the golden pecan."

"If you lost consciousness, it could lead to a brain injury."

"Darlin', I'm fit as a fiddle. You're worrying too much lately. Everything seems to be upsetting you. I think you need to lay off that Marie Kondo stuff. It might spark joy in you when you straighten something out, but now you get all heated-up when you see messy things. Some of the best parts of life are the messy things. Don't you know that?"

"That's not true. My life is more organized than ever. Tidying up has made me feel empowered. I do admit it's a bit like a drug. You can't stop once you start."

Maggie shook her head, causing the ice in the bag she was holding to jiggle. "Betsy darling, it's important to find the joy in life, and I don't mean reorganizing the garage. I know it sounds cliché but sometimes you do have to stop and smell the roses. Don't worry about what might happen but concentrate on the wonderful things happening in front of you right now. If you're going to worry about anybody, worry about that beautiful family of yours. Your aunt Maggie is doing fine."

"I'll be the judge of that," Dr. Morton said as he entered the room. He took a small flashlight from his white jacket pocket and held it up to Maggie's eyes. He turned to me for a second and smiled. "Hello, Betsy, here to check on your aunt?"

Maggie shifted the bag of ice to her lap. "Reports of my death have been greatly exaggerated."

"I heard she was at death's door, Dr. Morton."

The doctor flipped the light to the other eye. "Well, then, I have some bad news for you, Betsy. I think your aunt's going to outlive us all. Looks like she just bumped her head."

"Wonderful," I said.

"I told you." Maggie gave me a stern look. Her gaze shifted back to the doctor. "When can I go home?"

"Your eyes look good, but it might be prudent for you to spend the night so our staff can keep an eye on you."

Aunt Maggie scowled and began to scoot off the bed. "Not today, doctor. I'm in the middle of the Golden Pecan Treasure Hunt. I need to get back to my team."

"I should've known. We've had a run on accidents today. People are spraining ankles and coming in dehydrated in this heat."

As much as Maggie wanted to continue the treasure hunt, an extended stay might be good for her. "If you think she should stay here overnight, doctor, I will make sure that she does." Maggie shot me another look.

Dr. Morton sighed. "I don't know. This really is a minor injury. Will you have somebody around you at all times?"

"Yes. I'm on a team with Ruby Green."

"Well, I should probably keep you here, but as long as you stay with somebody the entire time, I think you'll be fine. The minute you start feeling dizzy or nauseous, you stop. You promise me?"

Aunt Maggie put a hand over her heart with the allegiance of a brand-new Cub Scout. "I promise."

I wasn't sure the doctor's decision was a good one, but I knew I needed to keep an eye on her from here on out. "I'll drive you home so you can check on Danny. Leo's probably ready to get back to the treasure hunt."

"A quick trip before that?" Maggie asked.

"I don't know..." I said, thinking Maggie already looked tired.

"Humor me. I'm injured. I want to run by the police station to see if anyone else has been knocked out."

"And you could also press charges on Bosco."

"I told you later. I thought about calling over there but we're in the throes of competition, darlin'. Loose lips sink ships. Someone could be listening in on the party line."

I decided not to tell her party lines hadn't been in existence for forty years, and just like the doctor, I easily succumbed to her will.

Ten minutes later, we stood talking to Dad at the Pecan Bayou Police Department. Lieutenant Boyle was standing near the back, his customary dark suit jacket off as he slogged down a bottle of water.

My father leaned over the counter, holding a file folder. "Well, Maggie, it seems you're the only victim at present. You sure you can't give me any more details?"

"I'm not even sure myself. Maybe I fell, but I do have my suspicions and the notebook I was carrying around is missing."

"That's interesting. If someone did push you down, who might that be?" Boyle asked, coming up for air.

She leaned forward and whispered, "Bosco Brown, the brute. That man is trouble."

"So, you say, sister." My dad's hesitance was obvious from the way he began touching the ends of his mustache, a maneuver I'd seen many times. "I haven't seen enough of him to make a judgment as of yet."

"Take my advice, Judd," Maggie said. "Whatever is stinkin' in Pecan Bayou, you can just bet he'll be at the root of it."

"I've seen guys like that all my life. If they're not in trouble, they're looking for it," Boyle added.

Vic Butler stepped into the lobby of the police station, and cleared his throat. "Judd, I'm glad I found you. Sarah's gone missing."

"Missing? What do you mean? We just saw her a few hours ago."

"Yes, but—" He focused on the handkerchief he was holding, appearing to avoid eye contact with anyone."

"That was before."

Boyle joined my father at the counter.

"Before what?" Maggie asked.

The last time I spoke to Vic Butler, he had given his wife Sarah something to sleep. It seemed like over-medicating to me, but I wasn't married to the woman.

He stammered. "Sarah has a problem."

"You mean other than flirting with my son?" I

I know it sounded cold, but every time I thought of Tyler and that woman together, I knew it had the potential to get out of control fast.

"This is the first we've heard of that," Boyle said. "Your wife is a real looker, but I never knew she was flirting with anyone else. That's why I've always been single. The mind of a woman is the only case I'll never solve. Funny, your wife never made a play for me." From the looks on the faces of the other people in the room, Boyle was the only one who was surprised by this fact.

"Don't judge a woman just because she has good taste. Seriously, though, a woman your wife's age going after my grandson. You could have some pretty big problems. Has she done this type of thing before?" Dad asked.

Vic straightened. "Of course not. She isn't like that, and frankly I'm insulted you would insinuate such a thing. The flirtation thing is minor. She's not good with people and sometimes she goes overboard without realizing it. For your information, Sarah has somnambulism."

"She has what?" Maggie asked.

"She's a sleepwalker," I said.

Vic gave me a grateful smile. "She took some medication and was at home sleeping when I last saw her. Now she's gone. I'm afraid she walked away while in a state of heavy sleep. And I hate to say it, but she can be extremely dangerous when she's like this. Her eyes will be open, and she will see people, but she doesn't see them for who they are. They take on the characters in her dream. She might see you or she might see a monster she feels is threatening her. Can you have your officers search for her?"

"I'm on it," Dad said. "Our fill-in dispatcher is taking a lunch break, but I think I can make an all-call."

Dad walked over to Prim's dispatch desk and began announcing to the officers on duty to keep an eye out for Sarah Butler. After finishing his official announcement, he turned back to us. "I have to go and chase after these golden nut fools, but we'll be looking for Sarah while we're out there."

"Thank you." Vic pulled a business card out of his pocket. "Call me if you hear anything. This is my cell number."

"Is there anything I can do to help?" I asked.

"She's very vulnerable when she's like this. Thanks." He handed me a card as well. He was such a kind man and so concerned for his wife. Pulling me aside, he whispered. "There is one little thing you could do for me."

I nodded, curious as to why he would pick me.

"I need you to get into Mark Valencia's store. You have a reputation for figuring out crimes in this town. Sarah is terrified it was Bunny who killed Mark and feels like she could be next. You have an eye for detail. I've been reading your wonderful columns on organization, and well, this is something that needs to be...organized. Could you look around the store one more time? Maybe you'll see something the police haven't. Getting this murder solved would be a huge relief for my wife."

"Why don't you do it yourself? I mean, I'm flattered, but I don't think the police will have missed much. My dad is pretty thorough."

"Yes, but they don't see things the way you do."

So basically, Vic wanted me to help his wife and disregard the fact she was flirting with my son, a naïve high school senior. He continued to watch me, waiting for an answer. "I guess I could take a look around." I never was good at saying no.

Maggie started coming toward us, so Vic began to speak quickly. "Thank you so much. My priority is finding Sarah safe. If you can help catch this killer, it will give her some much-needed peace of mind."

I shrugged. "No problem."

He placed a hand on my arm. "Thank goodness. Use those superior observation skills you were blessed with, and once again, you'll be helping our family."

As we exited the police station, Maggie announced, "Before I join Ruby, I want to find that Bosco Brown and give him a piece of my mind. She texted me and says she's getting off her feet in the air conditioning for a half hour. She never found Bosco, but I sure will."

"Are you sure that's wise?" Not only would it stir up trouble, but it would put us all even further behind in the treasure hunt. "Leo and Danny are waiting. We could help you hunt him down after the contest."

"I'm sure." She marched to the car with all the might of someone of small but mighty stature. Hell hath no fury like Aunt Maggie on a roll. Leo had texted while we were at the police station telling me he went ahead and walked Danny back to our house. I grabbed my cell and typed out an update.

My phone beeped. Reading the text aloud, I said, "Leo said he saw Bosco and Earl go into the coffee shop. He'll meet us there."

"And Danny?"

"He's fine."

"Thank goodness. And that's perfect. I'm feeling under-caffeinated after all those needles in the hospital. I can get a cup of java and the chance to square up against a bully. Two birds, one stone."

"Aunt Maggie, stop. You will do no such thing. I promised Dr. Morton we will look after you. That doesn't include a slap-down with Bosco Brown."

"I always taught you bullies were not to be toyed with. I'd be living a lie if I backed down now," Maggie said, walking surprisingly well for a woman who just left the emergency room.

I loved this woman more than anything, but she could be the definition of stubborn. "Don't overdo it, Aunt Maggie."

"I can take care of myself," she snapped.

My thoughts drifted to the possibilities of juggling taking care of her, along with everything else on my schedule. It could create the very chaos that Marie Kondo warned against. I would have to totally redesign my bullet journal if I had to add Maggie's infirmity into it. Perhaps I was being cold, but I firmly believe the expression *fail to plan and plan to fail*. If she needed me, no matter what was going on in my life, I would be there for her and for Danny. Maggie was potentially forcing me to revise my plan, and I found that unsettling.

When we approached the coffee shop, Leo was leaning against the brick wall underneath the hanging sign that displayed a cup of steaming coffee with Earl's Java lettered boldly above it.

"Are you okay?" Leo straightened himself and bent over to touch the arm of my diminutive aunt.

"I'm fine. Sure, I'm a little stiff, but old bones don't always cooperate. You'll find that out someday. It's all mind over matter anyway."

Maggie glanced past him into the coffee shop. Earl was behind the counter, and we could see Bosco sitting at a booth, with clues spread out in front of him. On the corner of the table was Aunt Maggie's notebook. We could hear his loud voice through the window as he and Earl shared a laugh.

"Easy as pie," he said as we entered the shop.

Earl placed a coffee filter into a machine and grinned at his brother. "I knew we could do this. Coming right up—a chocolate caramel coconut mocha, Bosco's signature drink."

"Hell to the yes. These yocals don't have a clue when it comes to finding money," Earl boasted, his chest puffing out a bit.

"Bosco," Maggie said, positioning herself square in front of the booth where Bosco sat, holding her pocketbook in such a way that I wasn't sure whether she planned to use it as a weapon. "I'm not exactly sure what happened, but I think you need to know..."

Vic walked through the door, interrupting, "Has Sarah been in, Earl?"

"No," Earl answered. "I think I'd remember that."

Vic nodded. "If you see her, will you give me a call?" He walked over and plopped a business card on the counter.

"Sure. Is everything okay?" Earl asked.

Vic gave a reassuring smile. "Just call if you see her. It's important."

As Vic left, Maggie tried to resume her discussion, but Bosco wasn't having it. "Yeah, yeah. I get it. You think I'm the reason you got banged up. News for you, lady. I did nothing to you. Now skedaddle and take this worthless notebook of yours. I found it laying on the ground. Maybe you should keep up with your stuff better. You old biddies are way behind. We're about to win this here treasure hunt."

A red cloud started up Maggie's neck and continued to her cheeks. "I will not skedaddle. Not for a minute, you big bully." She eyed the clues spread out on the table and began to count to herself.

"You have two more clues than we do," she said.

Bosco moved his meaty arms over the compiled clues. "Big deal. Move on, lady. I can't help it that you and your biddy buddy can't keep up." Bosco glanced up at Earl. "Hurry up with that coffee. I need to get my creative juices flowing."

Before Earl could respond, Maggie leaned forward, intent on slapping Bosco. Thinking fast, I grabbed the notebook, and Leo took her by the elbow, guiding her out of the coffee shop.

"Don't start up with him, Aunt Maggie. There are some people you just can't reason with."

Even though I attempted to speak calming words to my aunt, I had to admit I was still angry after seeing Bosco's spread on the table. As we stepped out of Earl's, hearing the words "good riddance" behind us, Aunt Maggie quickly excused herself.

"Let's go find Ruby," Leo said, following behind us. "You don't need to waste your time with that guy."

"I can find Ruby on my own," Maggie replied, straightening her visor.

"I don't know," I said. "I told the doctor—"

"Yeah, I know what you told him, but that was just to get me out of that place. I promise you, I'm fine now. I'll text you when I get with Ruby. You two go off so you can get closer to finding the pecan than that gorilla in there. Ruby put this GPS thing on our phones, so we'd always know where the other one was."

She peered at the phone, trying to pull up the app, and then Leo gently pointed to an icon to push. "Thanks, Leo. I'm still stuck in the handheld calculator days, I guess. My division is great, but smartphones are still a mystery to me." Maggie held the phone in the air as if it were a torch in the night, following the signal to Ruby's location.

As Maggie marched down the street, I whispered to Leo, "We need to check out something. I made a promise to Vic Butler."

"Really?"

"I'll tell you all about it later," I answered, knowing he wouldn't be too happy we were about to go search a crime scene.

Chapter 12

When Leo and I got to Maximum Muscle, also known as the crime scene, we found the door open and Lieutenant Boyle standing inside with a clipboard. With the air conditioning flowing throughout the store, he had returned to his suit jacket with a white shirt underneath that was not quite tucked in properly.

"What are you doing here?" he asked, looking up from his work.

"I was wondering if you would mind us looking around the crime scene—for the newspaper?"

He pitched his head back slightly to the left, looking like he was not going to grant us entry. "Rocky was already here. Besides this isn't the kind of column you write. But the actual crime scene is the alley, not the store."

I had to think fast. I didn't think he even knew what I wrote, and searching the store definitely had nothing to do with providing helpful hints to the townsfolk of Pecan Bayou. "I know, but Rocky asked me to come back and take one more look around. He's afraid he might have missed something. A good journalist always double-checks his work."

Lieutenant Boyle gave me a suspicious nod. "Maybe I should check with your father."

"Oh, he knows about it," I lied. Even though I discouraged lying in my children, I justified it with the knowledge that if we did find something, we would inform the police.

He hesitated. "Okay. Take a look around, but don't touch anything. I'm sure you know that. "

"Thanks," I said, scurrying in before he could change his mind. Leo followed and gave Boyle an awkward wave as he made his way past him.

I headed to a backroom that was divided by a curtain made of fabric printed with buxom women in very skimpy clothing. It reminded me of the mud flaps on big-rig trucks.

Leo glanced at the curtains and grinned. "That's an inspiring room divider." He lowered his voice to a whisper. "I thought you said you were doing a favor for Vic, not Rocky. I think you need to explain why we're really here."

I surveyed the storeroom. It looked like Mark was a bit of a neat freak. Drawers and shelving containing stock were all labeled. There was a desk pushed against the wall with a clear calendar pad and invoices stacked neatly to the right. The one surprise was a cabinet door that was left open. Had he been about to retrieve something when the killer entered this area?

"Vic wanted me to look around and maybe see something the police haven't. Sarah's terrified the killer is Bunny and that she will come after her next."

"Seriously? Did you bring your x-ray vision glasses, or are you just going to use your photographic memory?"

"I'll have you know that Vic told me I have a reputation for solving crimes in this town. He also complimented me on my ability to organize and focus on small details. I'm a legend in this town, Leo."

"If you say so. I guess I should be proud my wife is considered some kind of super neat, crime-solving wonder."

"Well, thank you for that. I was a little surprised he asked me to do this, especially after what just happened with Tyler and Sarah," I said.

"Actually, I think the whole incident was pretty innocent. Tyler might have a crush on her, but if she seriously made a pass at him, he'd be terrified. Trust me."

"Really? I wish I felt that way. She's gorgeous. He's been leading with his hormones for years now. Self-control might be pretty tough in that situation."

"You don't give Tyler enough credit. He has plenty of self-control. He's not that kid who pushed Zach over at the scout meeting all those years ago, you know. He's almost a man. I think we can trust him."

"I remember that day. Tyler was twice Zach's size, and I was sure he was going to beat him up."

Leo pulled me close. "I remember that day, too. That was the first time I ever laid eyes on you. Nothing's been the same ever since." Maybe it was all the dormant testosterone in the air, but suddenly, the back room of Maximum Muscle seemed like a great place to try out our future cruise ship plans. As I kissed Leo, out of the corner of my eye was that open cabinet door. I slid my elbow back and closed it.

Leo pulled away, "Now? You're tidying up now?"

"Wait. Look at that cup." There was a disposable coffee cup from Earl's Java on the counter in the back room. I would think a weightlifter would want to stay off caffeine. Scribbled on the front were the words *chocolate caramel coconut mocha*, the exact same concoction Earl was whipping up for Bosco at the coffee shop.

"Take a look at that, Leo. Bosco has been back here. Wasn't that what he ordered at the coffee shop?"

"How would you know that?" Leo asked.

"Earl said it—it was the drink he was making for Bosco at the coffee shop. I guess it stuck with me because it's an unusual drink."

"Do you believe Bosco could have come back here to kill Mark and then left his coffee cup? I think if I were going to kill somebody, I would clean up after myself." I loved that Leo said that. Maybe some of my tidying up was rubbing off on him.

"I need to tell Dad about that." In the corner, I noticed a box of plastic water bottles Mark must've been saving to recycle. Just like me and an open cabinet that needed closing, if Bunny had been here, I had a hard time believing she would pass up this giant box of recyclables. Her mantra to save the planet was more than just words. It was her religion. She wouldn't be content leaving a large box of recyclables sitting here. Whether or not this desire would take precedence while murdering Mark Valencia was another thing. Bunny was a driven woman, and I was almost sure she would have picked up that box on her way out.

"Do you see anything else?" Leo asked.

"Nope." I walked to the computer on Mark's desk and after wiggling the mouse saw that the accounting software had been left on. The login page waited for the proper cue to start the program, with the last message being an incorrect password. Someone had been trying to log in but had failed. Had Mark forgotten his password, or had this been Bosco looking for a record of the transactions? Mark's personal calendar was nested under that. Using the theories of Marie Kondo, I would think too many open programs are just like a person who can't close a cupboard door.

Leo continued to search behind me. "I don't know if you should be touching that computer."

"I think it will be okay." Closing the apps, I shut down the computer. I joined Leo searching the room for another minute when Lieutenant Boyle popped his head through the curtain.

"You two have been back here long enough. Have you seen everything you wanted to see? "

"I guess so. Is there a list of things from this room considered evidence in the murder?"

"It's down at the station now. I do have a few things here. Just in case you were looking for it, the answer is yes, they did find a supply of steroids." He showed me the clipboard he had been carrying. I looked through the list, but there was no mention of women's possessions. "I still find it hard to believe that Mr. Valencia thought that there would be a market for this stuff in this town. He was actually selling steroids?"

"Well, I guess Pecan Bayou has to keep up with the times."

When we came out of the shop and headed toward the town square, Josiah and Prim were sitting on one of the lovely park benches the town council had provided. The plan was to try and encourage the small number of tourists we were blessed with each year. Fredericksburg got the bulk of the spring wildflower visitors, while Pecan Bayou was just another town along the way. Howard Gunther had suggested at several town council meetings that we should get an attraction like the world's largest ball of string.

"People will drive for miles to see that sort of thing. Just think of Ripley's Believe it or Not. Half that stuff is fake anyway." He was solidly voted down. Howard was still at a loss for respect after he tried to get the town listed in America's most haunted places because of our highly-spirited abandoned tuberculosis hospital. Our town's leaders wanted tourists to come to Pecan Bayou, but they wanted them to visit for the live people and amenities, not the dead ones.

Rocky Whitson was in conversation with Prim and looked happy to see me when we approached. Josiah was taking a quick nap, a little snore escaping his lips.

"It's not good to be sitting out in this heat," Leo said, speaking in his official weatherman voice.

Prim crossed her arms, giving her husband a frustrated look. "Try telling that to Mr. I-know-it-all here. He was afraid if we went inside somewhere, we might miss watching other teams who seem to be ahead of us."

"How many clues do you have?" I asked. There was a stack of yellow clue papers in Josiah's hand.

"We're up to the three sisters, but for the life of me I can't figure out what that's all about."

Prim shook her head while Rocky appeared to hold back a giggle. "One of my better ideas," he said.

"I don't think anyone else in town thinks so," I said, wanting to quash Rocky's enthusiasm for his own deviousness.

"Uh-huh." That was it. Rocky wasn't talking even if I did insult him.

Leo removed his ball cap and then readjusted it. "We just ran into Bosco and Earl at the coffee shop. I think they're ahead of all of us. I'm not even sure how many clues they've figured out, but Bosco had them spread out on a table. We can't let someone who doesn't even live here win this thing. It just wouldn't be right."

Prim grimaced. "That man. I've been going to Earl's Java for years, and if I had known he had a brother like Bosco, I'd have switched to drinking tea."

I rubbed the back of my neck. "I worry for Earl. I think a lot of people are choosing not to stop in because of Bosco."

Josiah opened one eye. "What's that you say? Bosco Brown has more clues than we do? That can't be. I've spent the last six months analyzing every aspect of this race. What has Bosco done but sit in prison?"

I hated to tell Josiah but sitting behind bars could also give a man time to think.

Prim patted her husband on the arm. "Calm down, Josiah. You know your blood pressure can act up in the heat like this."

Josiah pressed his lips together. "Yes, dear. I'll be careful."

Leo pointed to a red cooler that had been set up on the steps of the old white gazebo. "Why don't you go get yourself a bottle of water at the gazebo?" There was a cautionary sign written on poster board placed in front of it.

For the Treasure Hunters
AND NO ONE ELSE

I recognized the personal touch of Mayor Obermeyer, who would never provide free water to the general public and was always clear in expressing his opinions. He probably had to be coerced to provide this amenity. His theory was that if you were going to hunt for treasure, come prepared and do not depend on government largesse to provide water.

Prim grabbed her husband's pudgy hand. "Sounds like a grand idea." As she started to pull him off the bench toward the gazebo, but Josiah pulled in the other direction.

"How about a cup of coffee at Earl's instead?" With the temperature in the high nineties and a generous portion of humidity blanketing us, coffee sounded like a terrible idea to me.

"In this heat? You must be crazy." As Prim started to protest more, a smile played at her lips. "Oh, I get it. You want to see if you can read over Bosco's shoulder and get a free clue, right? We'd be doing exactly what Earl and Bosco did to Rocky when he wrote up the clues."

He winked at Prim and made a clicking sound with his mouth. "That's my girl."

Rocky pitched his head back slightly in surprise. "They were looking over my shoulder? I should have known 'free refill' in Pecan Bayou is never really free."

"At least you know they didn't see everything, or they would have found the golden pecan by now," Prim said in a comforting voice.

Josiah offered his arm to his wife. "So, we're off to get coffee and clues."

"Fine, but first I need something cold. Let's get some water and then make our way over," Prim said.

"I think I'll join," Rocky said. "Now that I know they were attempting to cheat, I want to see what Bosco's up to."

"Just one more thing before you go, Prim. Do you know anything about Bosco Brown's criminal record?" I asked.

Rocky gave me an appreciative look, and he reached into the pocket of his shirt for his reporter's pad.

Prim dabbed at a bead of sweat on her temple. "I believe he was in the pen for an armed robbery over in Round Rock. Something he did several years ago. He served his time. It doesn't mean he hasn't been a suspect in lots of things around here, starting with shady dealings that center around Mark Valencia. I suppose now that poor Mr. Valencia has been murdered, it will be easier to prove these connections. I'll tell you what, if Bosco is behind that man's murder, your daddy will nail him for it."

It was becoming evident that Bosco was our man, and if we connected the drink cup we saw in the Maximum Muscle backroom, we could firmly place him at the murder scene.

"Do you know where he was at the time of the murder?" I asked.

Prim gave a knowing nod. "At the time of the murder, Earl said he was setting up a team of temporary workers in the coffee shop. Bosco said he couldn't remember. At least that's what he told your father. No witnesses, of course."

"That's pretty weak. So, Bosco doesn't have an alibi, then." Once more, Bosco was riding the top of my suspect list. This would put Bunny in the clear even if she was wielding a shotgun at anyone who graced her front porch. How had the Thatchers fared with her?

"How did you do over at Bunny's house?" I asked.

Josiah, looking to be suffering in the heat, pulled a white cotton handkerchief out of his pocket and wiped his brow. "We got out of there just in time. That woman is crazy. Thought she was going to kill us."

Before Josiah could catch a breath to keep talking, Prim continued the story. "Judd got over there and took her gun away, thank God. Bless her heart. She isn't the same after what happened to her sweet sister, although I must say it was kind of strange with her out in the middle of the night like that—"

"But to jump off that bridge and hit her head the way she did. Very sad," Josiah said, finishing his wife's sentence. "I bet you haven't heard all the rumors."

"I don't know if you should share that, Josiah," Prim said, suddenly pulling out of their shared track of communication. Josiah continued.

"I heard she was having a romantic tryst," he said, undeterred by his wife's nudging.

As if we were on a ship listing with the sea, Leo and I leaned in the direction of Mr. Thatcher. "Who with?" I asked, trying to remember Bunny's sister being romantic with anybody. She was what my aunt would have labeled as plain. Pale skin, no mascara, hair that had never seen a curling iron. That being said, she was a kind, lovely person who always greeted people on the street. It was news to me that Poppy Donaldson may have had a romantic rendezvous in the middle of the night.

Josiah Thatcher leaned back, his eyes checking out the action on the street. "I heard it from Lester Jibbets, who heard it from Glory McGiver after Pastor Green got on to Delta Haney for talking about it at the quilt group. So, you know it's pretty solid. You're not going to believe this, but..." He lowered his voice. "Some say it was Sarah Butler."

"Are you kidding me? Sarah and Poppy? An item?" Rocky asked.

"*No*." I was shocked. I sure didn't see that one coming. Sarah was a lonely woman, but I never suspected she and Poppy were an item.

"Come on," Leo said. My husband had a tendency to take gossip with a grain of salt.

"I know. It sounds outrageous," Mr. Thatcher said, "But the word is Sarah was walking around that night and met Poppy at the bridge. At least that was the direction that some people at Goin' Nuts saw her walking."

"Josiah, stop," Prim admonished. "It's just gossip. There's no evidence those two women were romantically involved. And what would it matter if they were a couple?"

He sighed and put his hanky in his pocket. "You're right, dear."

"In the dispatch office, I listen to people for a living. There's a lot more gossip than actual information going around. Maybe you should keep that to yourself," Prim scolded.

Josiah turned to Rocky, a purveyor of all things gossipy. "I could, but it's all over town. The nuts of Pecan Bayou can't stop talking about it."

Chapter 13

As the Thatchers made their way over to get water at the gazebo, Rocky tipped his ball cap. "I'd love to stay with you all day, but I need to check up on Bosco, and I have a first-class murder to write about. You haven't heard anything new, have you?"

I lifted my chin and smiled. "Nothing. Well, nothing I want to share for publication." I didn't want to reveal the many personal things I was learning about Sarah Butler, because Rocky could be a gentleman up to the point of WWED—What Would *The Enquirer* Do? I chose to keep it to myself.

Rocky gave me a look. "What's that supposed to mean? Are you hot on the trail of some sort of clue that doesn't involve reorganizing your closet?"

"Of course not, but have a heart, Rocky. When someone gets murdered, it's murder, not just the next above-the-fold headline, you know? I'm trying to figure it out like everyone else."

Rocky placed a hand on his chin and observed me for a moment. "Uh-huh." His phone beeped, and glancing at the screen, he said, "Nicholas wants me to call. Something about a missing person. We'll talk about this later."

With the heat closing in around us, Leo and I took the Thatchers' place on the bench. My thoughts drifted to Sarah. I hoped Vic would find her. For someone so put together on the outside, she was a mess on the inside. If we had x-ray vision enabling us to see what was really going on with people, I doubt we would ever leave the house. I tried to shift my focus back to the contest. "I can't believe Bosco has figured out the three-sisters clue. He doesn't even live in this town. How could a big brute like that have the shrewdness for strategy?"

Leo ran his hand through his damp hair, replaced his ball cap and leaned back on the bench. "Maybe the fact that he doesn't live here gives him the advantage."

"What do you mean by that?"

"Well, you and I based our deductions on what we know of the town's history. What if we didn't know who lived here? What if we had to rely on only what was presented before us? A man who's been in prison would have situational awareness, right?"

"I guess so."

I stretched and yawned, the heat making me sleepy. It made sense. If that was how he figured it out, then instead of focusing on actual sisters, I needed to think out-of-the-box about any groups of three. I looked around and counted the columns on the courthouse. Four. The stoplights downtown. One. The banners advertising the Golden Pecan Treasure Hunt. Two—one placed at the beginning of Main Street and one at the end. After that, I was hard-pressed to think of anything. Given my obsession with Marie Kondo, I should be automatically thinking about things organized in little groups, and yet I had no clue. I decided to become one with my environment and sat quietly, observing everything in the town square. Josiah and Prim were resting on the gazebo steps drinking from water bottles. Maggie and Ruby were coming out of the Best Little Hair House in Texas, talking, of course. Rocky was walking into Earl's. Everything was normal in Pecan

Bayou. Nothing seemed out of place. A second later, Bosco and Earl exited Earl's Java, Rocky hot on their trail.

There was more than one way to become one with my surroundings. It was time to tackle the problem head-on. I rose from the bench.

Leo jumped up. "What are you doing?"

"I need to ask Bosco a question." Leo placed his hand on my arm in an effort to hold me back.

"Are you crazy? I don't think he's feeling too neighborly right now."

Like that disorganized junk drawer I conquered last week, I needed to straighten this three-sisters thing out. I had tackled worse than Bosco Brown in my day, even if he was six foot four and 230 pounds of pure muscle. I was five foot four and 130 pounds of pure...motivation. I approached Bosco and Earl as they were about to cross the street.

"Bosco? Could I talk to you for a minute?"

Rocky gave me a great big "go ahead" grin. Betsy Fitzpatrick, girl reporter. "I was just talking to these gentlemen about Sarah Butler. Seems she's turned up missing."

Bosco, who seemed to propel himself by his muscled chest, stopped like a granite statue. "And I said we don't know nothing about it. Ain't that right, Earl?"

Earl nodded.

"I have a different question. One about the treasure hunt." His focus intensified on me, making me feel like a mosquito to be swatted away.

He grunted. "And what would that be?" As he scowled at me, it felt like my mosquito had turned to a cockroach discovered in the kitchen at midnight.

"We are having the hardest time figuring out the three-sisters clue. You see..."

He began to grin as I babbled on. He was enjoying this. This guy who was considered a reject of society six months ago now had people chasing after him for his expert opinion. He was clearly reveling in his new stature. He tapped on the side of his head.

"You have to use your noodle." He took me in with an appraising glance. "You're just so pretty I'll bet you don't have to use that part too much, but me? I'm thinking all the time."

I wasn't quite in agreement with his self-appraisal but decided to leave it alone for now. If I could keep him enjoying our conversation, maybe he would let something go about the three sisters. After the comments on my physical appearance, I needed to work fast because Leo was not going to put up with him saying things like that to me for very long.

I beamed at him like a kindergarten teacher looking at a crayon drawing. "I can tell you're thinking all the time. We've already tried to connect the one set of sisters in town to the clue, but it just didn't work."

He folded his arms like a regal king of medieval times. I expected to hear a bugle call in the distance. "All I'm going to tell you, little lady, is to open your eyes. Enjoy nature."

Earl gave an abrupt nod making a signal that our discussion was finished. "Times a-wastin' Bosco. We got to go."

"Oh, and one more thing," I said as both men stepped off in the other direction. "What were you doing in Maximum Muscle?"

Rocky almost fell off the curb. Bosco turned around and I was sure I saw his demeanor change. "Why do you think I was in Maximum Muscle?"

"Caramel, chocolate, and coconut. You're the only one I know who orders that mixture of coffee, and we found your empty cup in the back room. So again, I ask, what were you doing there? Were you doing some kind of business with Mark? Did something go wrong?"

Bosco's bottom lip curled. "I don't know what you're talkin' about."

Leo stepped forward. "But you *were* doing business with Mark Valencia, weren't you?"

"What's it to you? And before you ask me the next part, yes, I do have an alibi."

Rocky stepped over next to me, creating a unified front. "What?"

"I'd rather not say. It's personal."

"Not good enough," Rocky said. "We're talking murder here. We have a killer walking loose among the citizens of Pecan Bayou. Your alibi is going to have to be public knowledge, especially with your record."

"Public knowledge?" The big man paled.

Leo stood behind me, putting his arm around my shoulder in a proprietary way. "And if you don't want to go back to prison—"

Earl blew out an exasperated sigh, clearly impatient with our impromptu questioning. "All right. Fine. I'll tell you. He was getting a boil taken off his butt down at Dr. Lee's office. Heard enough, or do you want pictures?"

"Do you have a clear shot—" Rocky started but I cut him off.

"Thanks," I called after Earl and Bosco as they walked away from us. Bosco took on an embarrassing slump after the disclosure of his emergency medical procedure.

"I guess even big guys like Bosco get boils on their butt," Leo said. "Sort of levels life's playing field for the rest of us, doesn't it?"

"I have to get to the Gazette," Rocky scowled. "And you, young lady. Keeping back important information like finding that cup in Maximum Muscle. When were you going to tell me about that?"

"I wasn't sure it was anything. I'm still not sure. Just because I find something out doesn't mean I want it in the paper."

Rocky looked shocked. I had taken the name of cheap sensationalism in vain. "You really don't have ink in your blood."

"Nope, and sometimes I think you need a transfusion of the red stuff every once in a while. Are you going to put in the paper that Bosco was getting a boil removed?"

Rocky's eyebrows rose. "Of course not. I'm not a monster, you know. I'll just say he was having surgery on his derriere. Sounds good, using French like that. Half the town will think he was having surgery at the ice cream shop."

As Rocky walked away, I realized that Bosco's fairly solid alibi shook me. I was sure he was our murderer. He was a big burly guy with an attitude and a prison record. How could he not be the murderer? Now I had to go back to square one.

Thirty minutes later Maggie, Ruby, Leo, my father, and I sat around our kitchen table. "Well, that's that," I said. "There is no way Bosco Brown could have been the murderer." None of us were getting any further with the clues to the hunt or Mark's murder, so I decided it would be best if we came together to share information. Aunt Maggie and Ruby had agreed as well as my father, who was glad to be out of the heat.

"I just wish Mr. Bosco Brown would have shared that with the police department," my father said. "You would think a man who is coming off a prison sentence would want to be nothing but honest with the police. It boggles my mind what ex-cons do."

Leo, who was about to sink his teeth into a ham sandwich, suppressed a grin. "I think this would be a good time to practice understanding. Give the guy a break."

Aunt Maggie bristled. "Give him a break my foot. He has been nothing but a bully this whole time, and the fact that he got a little bit embarrassed doesn't bother me one iota. I guess karma got him for pushing over an old lady."

While we discussed Bosco, I kept my eye on Coco in the next room playing with her dollhouse. After our last unfortunate experience with the paint on the wall, she seemed subdued. I felt calmer now that everything was back in its place. The walls had been cleaned, and my daughter also seemed to be where she should be. Zach had put Butch in the tub, so his tail had returned to its natural shade. As Marie said, it is important to find a moment of joy in all the chaos the world has to offer. I could only hope that my good luck would continue. I turned my attention back to the adults.

"The thing is," I said. "If it's not Bosco, then who?"

Ruby piped up. "She's your little detective, Judd. She just can't leave a mystery alone. You'd think with all this deductive reasoning, she would have found the golden pecan by now."

My father gave me a patient smile. "Yes, but this time I know she will restrain herself," he said, giving a side look not unlike the one I just gave Coco.

"But, Dad—" I was about to go into a persuasive argument that would change his mind immediately.

"Don't you 'but Dad' me," he said, wadding up his napkin. "This is a police matter."

This wasn't the first time my father had made an effort to keep me out of his business. I would try, but he always needed me in the end. He couldn't deny that. "Okay, if this is a police matter, let me ask you as a concerned citizen—just who else you have in mind?"

Coco came running in, holding a hair fastener. "Did it come out again?" I asked as she placed it in my hand. This had become an attention-getting ritual with my daughter. Whenever she felt bored, she pulled out her hair fastener and asked me to fix it.

Ruby pulled her chair over. "Don't forget there's a hair professional in the room. Come over here, Coco."

Coco beamed at Ruby's indulgence. "Thank you, Aunt Ruby."

Ruby deftly took hold of the hair elastic, but before placing it in Coco's hair, she reached down and put her arms around my daughter, giving her a squeeze. "I can't tell you how much

I love hearing that, baby girl." She pulled the strands of Coco's hair up, placing it into a ponytail. "Oh, to have hair like this again." She looked over at me. "How much longer are you going to let it grow before you trim it?"

"From the amount of work it's getting to be, it won't be long now," I said.

Coco pouted. "No. I want my hair as long as a Disney princess."

"Spoken like a person who doesn't have to brush her own hair," Leo said. Yes, in this household, even dads had to take a turn at the snarls and tears.

"Go on and play now," I said.

"Mom—"

"You heard me."

She continued. "I wanted to ask Grandpa if he would help me take off my training wheels."

My dad reached over and tweaked her nose. "Not today, munchkin. I'm busy with this treasure hunt. Can you take a rain check?"

"What's that?" Coco asked.

I stood and turned her by the shoulders to face the living room. "Never mind, we'll get those training wheels off eventually. I promise."

"You already said that." She pouted again.

"And I meant it. Now go and play."

She turned around and left the room, her ponytail bobbing.

"Now," I said, returning to the business at hand. I zeroed in on my father, who was in the middle of crunching into a potato chip. "Who are you thinking about as your next suspect?"

"And you are asking me this as a concerned citizen. Is that how you put it?"

"Precisely," I said, pleased he wasn't shutting me down yet.

"Yes, we're all concerned," Maggie agreed, strengthening my public inquiry. I gave her a smile.

He used his napkin and then said, "Bunny Donaldson. She definitely had the motive, and I hate to say it, but after taking her shotgun away, I'm beginning to think that she was just crazy enough."

"I do believe you're right about Bunny being crazy, but I don't see her committing murder for the environment," Ruby added.

The walkie-talkie my father had placed on the table began to buzz. "Attention all units, we have a suspected shooting at the residence of Bunny Donaldson."

"Damn. She must have had another gun. And that's my cue to exit." Dad rose from the table. "This may just be the answer to all of your questions."

He was getting away before I could delve deeper into his theories on Bunny. "Be sure to keep us in the loop."

He turned with a mischievous smile. "Don't I always?"

After everyone left to resume the treasure hunt, Leo helped me clean up and then waited as I put dishes in the dishwasher and straightened the counters back to their originally organized glory.

"Are you finally finished?"

"I know this takes time, but in the end, you're going to thank me because you now have a neat house. It takes just a few minutes to organize something, and then you can reap the benefits and go about your day enjoying clutter-free living."

"Great." The enthusiasm of his words did not reach his voice. It was obvious the prospect of having a neat house up against a wife who can't stop cleaning was beginning to wear on him. "Can we go now? I've been thinking of some ideas for the three sisters. In a group of three, right?"

"What have you come up with?"

"Well, nothing specific, but I thought we might just drive around town and see if we can see something in a group of three. Part of my job is observing anything out of the ordinary. Sometimes you can't see an anomaly in your observations until you really start looking at things on a minuscule level. That's what we're going to do. We're going to put on our scientific hats and drive through town looking for any groups of three."

Take it down to the small details. This idea was just short of genius. We had been way too big-picture up until now. After making sure Coco would be supervised, I felt like home was under control. We headed out again with Leo's idea giving us new inspiration. If Bosco and Earl could figure it out, I was sure we could. We drove up and down the streets, counting trash cans, yard statues, even real estate signs. Every time we found anything of there were three of, we would search the area for a clue box, looking anywhere for the telltale yellow papers flapping in the wind.

"I don't know if this was such a good idea," Leo said, sounding discouraged.

"No, it's a great idea. We just have to stick with it. I know we're going to figure this out. Let me text Maggie and see if she's gotten any further." I quickly sent a message her way, and she reported they were at the community church where everything was in threes. Even so, they weren't having any luck. They had resisted going over to Bonnie Donaldson's house, and I was pretty proud of myself for putting it off, but after counting trash cans for twenty minutes, the idea of going on there was becoming quite a temptation.

"Let's drive down Bunny's street," I said.

Leo raised an eyebrow. "Wouldn't it be wiser to stay out of your father's hair while he's trying to deal with Bunny?"

"Yes, but I'm sure it's all over by now. Who knows what we might learn," I assured him.

"Well, I guess it wouldn't hurt anything, and we're not coming up with the answer to the three sisters, anyway." I was shocked Leo gave in. When we drove down Bunny's street, the canopy of beautiful elm trees provided much-needed shade to the cozy street.

Leo parked a few houses down, as Bunny stood in front of her home, arms stiff to her side, fists clenched. My father stood in front of her. "I didn't do anything that was against the law except protecting my property. Read the statutes, Judd. I have not broken any law."

"Miss Donaldson, we've been going through this for the last half hour, and I'm not arresting you. I'm telling you just because somebody crosses your lawn doesn't mean you have the right to shoot them without provocation."

"Just a minute, let me get one of them digital recording gadgets so that I can get down that you have threatened my Second Amendment rights."

Leo began to laugh. "He has his hands full with her. I would hate to have to go up against that crazy eco-terrorist."

Curious neighbors, treasure hunters, and several children were watching the entire exchange. We found a place to stand on the edge of the neighbor's lawn under the shade trees. After such an active day, and our quick lunch, I was starting to get a little tired. I spotted a dip between two of the lower branches in the tree and attempted to sit on it. When I did, I spied what looked like a camouflage cover over a small yellow slip of paper. Jumping up suddenly, I uttered, "Oh my God."

"What?" Leo rose suddenly. "Is it a bug? Did a bug land on you? Where is it?"

I motioned to him from where I was standing. "Come back here and look at what I'm looking at."

A couple of other bystanders also followed my words and backed up.

There, hidden among three beautiful elm trees—two in the front and one in the back—was a camouflaged clue box. We had found the three sisters.

Leo rushed over and picked up a piece of yellow clue paper and began to read.

You have found the sisters one, two, three
And now you are almost free.
Follow the clues where it's cold and dank
And put that cruise trip money in the bank.

Leo turned to me. "There's a clue box at the bank?"

"Maybe, but what around here is cold and dank? It certainly isn't the bank. It does rhyme nicely, though."

The other contestants who had been watching the Bunny scene now riveted their attention to us. We had finally solved the clue, but because I jumped up, everyone else found out about it too. Prim and Josiah came running up, waving their cell phones in the air. I hadn't even seen them watching Bunny and my dad.

"Word has it you found the three-sisters clue. We were down the street."

Any chance of an advantage we might have had was ruined. Thanks to the popularity of texting in Pecan Bayou, everybody was now on an even playing field. Aunt Maggie and Ruby came riding upon a scooter-round.

"You found it. I knew you'd figure it out. Was this that deductive reasoning you use when you're solving a crime?" Ruby sounded very impressed with me.

"Not quite."

Leo smiled. "She was sitting on it."

Ruby gave me a wink. "Whatever works, Betsy."

Many of the treasure hunters began to read the clue themselves, their lips moving to the words. "We're off to the bank," Ruby said. A stream of exhausted clue hunters headed in the direction of the Pecan Bayou State Bank.

"Here we are again with a clue we can't decipher." Leo rubbed the back of his neck. "If it's the final clue, do you think Bosco and Earl must have figured it out by now?"

That was a good question, and something I feared myself. They had been ahead of us all along. Now that we were near the end, we would have to outthink them and outrun them. "If they've figured it out, we would have heard the church bells ringing to announce the winner. No, I think they're just as stuck as we are, which brings us back to what in town is cold and dank."

We started listing off several possibilities such as walk-in freezers, basements—of which there weren't that many in town—and the archival room at the library.

"What about that one mausoleum in the cemetery? That's cold and dank," I suggested, although hoping that wasn't the answer.

"Maybe. I say we don't follow the crowd to the bank," Leo said.

"I agree. I know Rocky well enough to know he would never do something as easy as feature the actual place in the clue. That just makes it too easy. You wouldn't suppose Rocky would put a clue box in a mausoleum in the cemetery?"

Leo chewed on his bottom lip. "Maybe? It would be a great place to hide a clue. The clue box would be hidden by the mausoleum itself. Also, who visits a mausoleum unless they know the person inside?"

"True, but how would the caretaker feel about all of Pecan Bayou trudging through his cemetery?" If Rocky had done something like put a clue in the cemetery it would not go over well if anyone's flowers were knocked over.

Leo shrugged. "That is what it's there for, right?"

"So, we're off to the cemetery?" I dreaded the thought, but at least the trees would offer some shade.

"No, let's do that only if we absolutely have to. I think we should go to the library."

"The library?" Was the heat getting to him? We had already been at the library once today. If there had been a clue box, we would have seen it. "Why the library?"

"I know, I know. We were there before, but how about the archival room? That place is cold because it's temperature-controlled and the only people who ever go there are the genealogists."

"Sounds like a good idea."

So many of the regular library patrons were participating in the treasure hunt that I had to guess the library was as quiet as the mausoleum we were putting off visiting.

Chapter 14

"Here to check out a book?" Cora Jean, the librarian, sat behind the counter holding a dog-eared romance.

I grabbed the clue from Leo and held it up. "The last clue for the treasure lists something cold and dank. We thought about the archival room."

Cora Jean got a twinkle in her eye. "Does that mean the whole town's going to come in here in the next couple of hours looking for a clue box?" she asked, putting a bookmark in the paperback.

"Don't get too excited. Most people are going to the bank."

"And here I thought I would get even more unexpected visitors today. I usually hate working on Saturdays, but today it's downright fun. Do you know, did Mr. Butler ever find Sarah?"

"Not that we've heard."

The little librarian with the large round glasses leaned forward slightly, and using her best librarian voice whispered, "So sad about her. I had no idea she was a sleepwalker, and now I'm hearing she was cheating on her husband with Poppy Donaldson?"

Wanting to keep her talking, I commiserated. "He sure has his hands full. Had you ever heard about anything going on with Poppy before?"

"No, but it sure does explain a few things. You know I go play bingo every Thursday night at St. Mary's and I've seen her walking down the street a couple of times. I thought maybe she was lost or meeting someone. I could never figure out what was going on with that woman, but I guess now we know."

So, other people had seen Sarah wandering around in a sleepwalking state. We walked down the musty stairs to the archival room together.

There was no clue box.

"I guess I should have told you we weren't a part of the treasure hunt, but it's just so nice to have someone to talk to today. My Saturday regulars aren't here, and it's kind of lonely. I never thought I'd miss Lester Jibbets and his Saturday newspaper binge."

With no yellow clue box awaiting us in the archival room, I suggested we go to the bank.

"So now you think the clue is at the bank after all?" Leo asked.

"We're not going there for the clue. I want to see what has happened to Sarah."

The bank was one of the taller buildings in the downtown grid with towering glass windows and stately red brick. Stan and Howard came out, and I noticed a yellow clue paper folded in the pocket of Howard's Hawaiian shirt. Howard, who didn't always remember to put on deodorant, left a heavy odor of sweat behind him.

"It's not in there," Stan informed us. "A bunch of people have been through already. I don't think the bank's too pleased. All their free pens are gone."

"Thanks." I put my hand on the door. "We need to see a banker."

"Okay..." Stan said, looking confused at my statement. I was almost sure he would next ask me if we needed to borrow money from him.

Howard grabbed the sides of his shirt and started flapping as if trying to circulate the cool air around him. "I hate to go back out in that heat." We weren't too crazy about the flapping shirt, either.

We strode across the tiled floor to Vic Butler's office. Howard's body odor dissipated from my nostrils as we encountered a fruitier scent inside the bank. Even though he had the Venetian blinds closed, through the doorway, we could see he was on the phone, hunched over the desk. One of his filing cabinet drawers was pulled out, probably left open when the phone rang. We saw him pull a notepad out of the desk drawer and begin scribbling information on it.

As we got closer we overheard his side of the conversation. "Yes. I see. Thank you so much for calling. I really appreciate you checking the woods." He hung up the phone and straightened upon seeing us. "It's like she's disappeared. No one can find her. I can't sit here another minute. I'm going to walk around the town one more time."

"Before you go, we just wanted to let you know that we searched Maximum Muscle but didn't find anything."

Vic gave out an exhausted sigh. "Really? Nothing? Well, thank God, and thank you for doing that. It would have been so embarrassing if something Sarah left behind in a sleep state or even a waking state ended up on a police report. This town has enough to talk about. Sorry, I have to go."

"No problem. Just glad we could help," I said as he quickly exited the glassed-in office.

"Man, I can't imagine how worried he must be," Leo said. "If that was you wandering around half out of your head, I don't know how I would handle it."

We were still standing in Vic's office. I glanced at the notepad. "Hmm, it looks like he's checked off everywhere they've searched so far." I took the notebook and returned it to the desk drawer.

"Betsy. Don't do that. It's bad enough you're tidying up behind us every second of the day, but it's not your place to tidy up Vic's office."

"Sorry. I just couldn't help myself," I said as I quickly shut the open file drawer.

"Betsy!"

"Sorry. I'll stop." But I knew I couldn't stop. Once you start seeing the world in organized patterns, you want to make sure everything goes where it belongs. There's a reason why people say, "Put all your ducks in a row." It felt so good. It really was like a drug.

"So where to next?" I asked.

"I guess it's time to get our chill on in some mausoleums." Leo drew out the word *mausoleum* with a slightly vampirey voice.

My phone buzzed, and I looked at the screen as we got into the car. "It's Zach."

"Are you guys almost done?" he asked, sounding a little impatient.

"At this point, it's hard to tell. What's up?" Two words every parent says with the greatest of trepidation.

"Nothing really. I was just wondering if I could go out like Tyler did. Danny could watch Coco."

"By himself? What do you mean Tyler went out? Again? Where?"

"I don't know. One of his friends called, and he said that you said it was okay. It *was* okay, wasn't it?"

Even though his job was to stay home and help Zach take care of Coco and now Danny, Tyler had just pulled another fast one. Yes, it was Saturday, and yes, he was about to be a senior in high school, but I thought becoming a senior also brought a modicum of maturity. Leo had assured me Tyler was more mature than I gave him credit, but still. All I could think was I had been reading the wrong parenting books.

"Hold on," I put my hand over the phone. "Tyler took off," I said to Leo, who was staring absently at the clue.

"He did? Wasn't he supposed to be helping Zach?" Leo answered, distracted. I felt my blood pressure rising, but Leo's focus was on the clue so I couldn't be too critical.

"Yes. He told Zach we gave him permission to go and left him alone. We need to find that boy and straighten him out."

Leo curled in his bottom lip and flinched as he began to back out of the park. "I might have told him that if everything was in control, he could go pick up a friend and bring him back to the house."

"You what? I never said they could have friends over. You know how distracted they can get. Coco could wander off, and neither boy would know it for hours."

"Not unless she took a video game controller with her," Leo said, a little laugh in his voice. He stopped when I glared at him.

I returned to the phone. "What friend would he have gone to pick up?" I asked Zach, thinking maybe we could find Tyler and get him back to where he should be.

"Uh, Aaron? Demarcus? I don't know who he's been hanging out with this week. You know, it's summer, and he's been hanging out with a lot of people."

Our house had turned into a revolving door of young men and women in the last year. Tyler was a star athlete, so one week it was the football team, and the next week it was basketball, not to mention the cheerleaders bouncing all over the place. Parenting a teenager was a little like directing traffic with a blindfold on.

"Fine. We'll be there in five minutes," I said as I clicked off the phone in anger. "He's out of control, and he clearly played us. Of course, he didn't tell me about you giving him permission because he knew I wouldn't stand for it."

Leo, who didn't seem to be bothered by the incident, kept his eyes forward and said, "Betsy, he's seventeen. He's going to test the limits. Don't you think that after the exhaustive parenting we've put into him all these years that we should begin to trust him a little bit?"

Trust him? Responsible people didn't dump on their little brother and leave him with babysitting duty twice in one day. Responsible people called their parents and told them they were abandoning their duties.

"I know what you're saying makes sense, but it's the principle of the thing."

"Well, I don't think we have to worry about him," Leo started slowing down the car as we neared the Pecan Bayou bridge.

"Leo? We need to get home," I said, but he appeared to be ignoring me.

"I realize that, but I think I found him."

I followed his gaze to see Tyler with his hands on Sarah Butler's shoulders.

Chapter 15

"What on earth?"

We bounded out of the car. Sarah Butler was the friend Tyler had left the house to meet? Even though this looked suspicious at first glance, it certainly didn't look like a romantic tryst. Instead, Tyler spoke evenly, as if with a small child.

He raised a hand gently and pointed to the bayou. "It's okay, Mrs. Butler. There's no one in the water."

Sarah's eyes were wide with fear. She brought her hands up to her mouth in horror, seeing something none of the rest of us could. Tyler reached for her arm.

"But I have to save her," Sarah cried. "She's hurt. It's all my fault. I made a mistake." She started pulling away from Tyler.

Leo stepped forward. "Mrs. Butler? Are you okay?" He positioned himself on her other side.

Sarah looked up at him, her eyes childlike, and she screamed. "No! Get away!" She tried to free herself.

"Sarah," I pleaded. "It's just Leo. He won't hurt you."

"He's a monster. He is going to hurt the lady. I have to fight him."

"Mrs. Butler. That's my dad. He's not a monster," Tyler said.

Sarah suddenly stopped fighting and pointed to the water below. "She's hurt. Can't you see that? She could die down there." Her attention fell completely away from Leo. Whatever threat she had perceived from Leo had vanished. I found it interesting that she was frightened of him and not me. Did she associate the "monster" with a man? If she encountered Mark Valencia, had she seen him as a monster or a man?

My eyes went in the direction she was pointing. No one was in the water, but Bunny Donaldson was down by the bank holding a small trowel and a terracotta flowerpot.

Tyler shook his head, looking down. "I found her like this. She was standing on the railing when I walked up. I still can't believe she came down after I asked her. I thought she was going to jump for sure. I've never been so glad to see my parents catching me doing something wrong. I was going to Demarcus's house when I found her."

Bunny Donaldson trudged up from the bayou's edge. "What's wrong with her?" Bunny pulled off her gardening gloves and stowed them in the clay pot with her trowel. Bunny had placed a deep red poppy in her long blonde braid, making her look like a very old Disney princess. "Did some of that silicone finally go up a few inches to her brain?"

Tyler flinched. "Don't say that. Can't you see she's out of it?"

"I think she's sleepwalking. See if we can guide her to the car," I said softly.

Tyler, using even tones barely above a whisper, said, "Mrs. Butler. Let's get in the car, and we can go and get help for that lady down there, okay?"

Sarah stared at the ground beneath the bridge. "Okay."

As Leo and Tyler gently placed her in the back seat of the car, I reached into my bag and retrieved Vic's card to call him. He answered on the first ring.

"We found her."

He let out an audible sigh of relief. "Where?"

"On the Pecan Bayou bridge. She thinks someone is in the water. She's not awake, but she's talking. I think I understand what somnambulism looks like now. Anyone seeing her would think she's fully awake."

"Thank God you found her," he said, his words breaking. "Can you bring her home to our house? I can meet you there."

"Of course," I said.

"I know where it is," Tyler offered.

"He does?" Vic asked overhearing him.

"He's the one who found her," I said. "This is going to be upsetting to hear, but she was about to jump off the bridge. I think she was trying to save Bunny Donaldson, who was planting a flower on the banks of the Bayou. Our son talked her out of it."

"Remind me to thank that young man. We need more like him around here." Vic hung up.

What was that? He wanted to thank our son for leaving his little brother to babysit so he could search for someone else's wife? Even though that was what I felt when we drove up to the bridge, Vic's words made me see the situation a little differently. I had been negative toward Tyler, but like Leo said, we needed to trust him more. He had saved a woman's life and was aware enough to see she wasn't in her right mind.

Before we could get the car started, Bunny Donaldson blurted out through the open window, "I think she's returning to the scene of the crime. Guilt will eat you up just like the rotten core of an apple. And what's that on her dress? By jingo, Sarah Butler may be a serial killer."

I craned my neck around to look at Sarah. We had been so focused on getting her off the bridge that I hadn't noticed her clothing. She had what appeared to be blood spots on the front of her red dress.

It was bad enough Vic was dealing with Sarah walking around town half awake. He didn't need the gossip mill adding "serial killer" to the conversational stream.

"We don't know that," I scolded. "We don't even know how whatever it is all over her dress got there. Be reasonable, Bunny." Bunny gave me a sideways scowl showing me she had no plans to curb her tongue.

"You want me to be reasonable when my best friend, my sister, and one of the few people in this town who will talk to me has been brutally murdered while I'm standing here right in front of the murderess? You have no idea what it's like to be me."

"You're right, I don't. But we need to get Sarah out of here right now." I rolled up the window.

Through the glass, Bunny shouted, "Sure, sure. We all have to protect the beautiful wife of the president of the bank. But of course, that's how things work in this town. The bigger your coconuts are, the more respect you get."

I looked over at Tyler, who was beginning to blush.

"Mark my words. I will see justice done. Until then, I will continue to come to the banks of Pecan Bayou and plant flowers in my sister's memory. This town will be drowning in poppies before I'm done."

Even though Bunny Donaldson was a royal pain in the behind, I was beginning to feel sorry for her. She was right. No one in town ever wanted to talk to her. But then again, why should they when she constantly berated people for ruining the planet. She spread guilt around like fertilizer on an ailing garden. The death of her sister made her lonely life even more burdensome.

I rolled down the window as Leo started driving. Just because she could be belligerent and rude didn't mean I had to be the same. "I don't know if I said this to you before, Bunny, but I am so sorry for your loss. I don't know what I would do without my family around me. They do mean the world to us, don't they?"

A tear formed in Bunny's eyes, and then it slipped down her pale skin. "That they do." With that, Bunny walked away, holding the clay pot next to her heart.

Pulling myself back to the problem of Sarah, I leaned back and tapped Tyler on the knee. "Tyler, Mr. Butler wants to thank you personally for what you did."

Tyler blushed. "It wasn't anything. I was walking to Demarcus's house, and there she was standing on the handrail of the bridge. She was wobbling like hell—"

"Tyler, language," Leo said.

"Sorry. Anyway, I could tell something was wrong and just started talking to her. I was really scared I'd say the wrong thing, and she'd jump."

"I know that had to have been scary for you," Leo said. "But you must have said the right thing, after all. Oh, and one more thing. The fact that you saved Mrs. Butler's life is wonderful, but you're still in trouble for dumping the babysitting duty on Zach...again."

"Really?"

"Yes, really. Coco can get into a whole lot of trouble if you don't watch her. You should know—"

"That's right," Sarah said, still in a trance. "She gets into trouble. That's why. That's why she was on the bridge. I'm so sorry. So sorry. Didn't mean..."

We were quiet for a moment as she drifted away. "What was that about?" Tyler asked.

I scratched the side of my head in thought. "I'm not sure, but I think it might have something to do with Poppy Donaldson."

I focused on the bloodstains Sarah had on the bodice of her dress. They were still bright red in some spots but drying. "I might not be a crime expert, but stains I know. That's blood."

"I don't know, but it's all over her," Tyler grimaced.

Vic met us in the driveway of his home. Leo and I jumped to help him with Sarah. She was still in a trance state but went along willingly with Vic. "Wait here, one minute. Will you?" he asked.

When he came back through the front door, he shut it quietly. "Thank you again. I can't tell you what a favor you've done for me...for Sarah today."

"Did you see the blood on her shirt?" Tyler asked.

"We need to call the police," Leo said.

Vic's shoulders stiffened. "No, we don't. Nothing bad has happened here. Your son saved her life. Celebrate that and let this be the end to it all."

Nothing bad happened? Was he being serious? His wife is walking around with blood on her dress and he was telling us it was a nothing to worry about. I was a little surprised at how quickly Vic was willing to let this go. It was as if he was trying to sweep it under the rug, making me think this was not the first time this had happened. Maybe he knew something about Poppy Donaldson's death? It was just a theory, but I had to try.

"Is this what you did after Poppy went over the bridge, and you knew your wife was involved?" I asked.

Vic's head jetted up. "Excuse me? I don't know what you're talking about, but if you are implying that my wife had anything to do with Poppy Donaldson's death, then you are way out of line."

His last statement proved to me that this was a secret Vic had been keeping to protect his wife. He loved her so much, I was sure he would lie about a suspicious death for her.

"When we walked up," I said, "Sarah was talking about how Poppy went over the bridge. She said she felt guilty about it and even said it was her fault. Could it be that Sarah was sleepwalking, and she and Poppy got into a physical altercation sending Poppy over the bridge to her death?"

Vic looked down, took in a breath, and then returned his gaze to mine. The coldness in his eyes surprised me.

"You'll never prove it."

"Are you saying she did it?" Tyler asked.

"Like I said, you can never prove it. Everyone knows that Poppy Donaldson's death was an accident. Even your own grandfather has put that in his report. You're young, but I think you can understand I love Sarah and will do anything to protect her."

"Even if she's responsible for somebody else's death? You would cover that up?" Leo asked.

"I need to see to Sarah—"

Before Vic could get his next word out, the Pecan Bayou Community Church bell rang in the distance. Someone had found the golden pecan.

"Damn. I need to be there," Vic swore.

"Is there somebody that you could call to watch Sarah?" I asked.

"Let me think," Vic said.

"Or we could have Tyler stay with her. I think she trusts him," I suggested. Leo gave me a questioning look. This was my way of extending trust to Tyler. He had been the one to find her. After what I had just seen on the bridge, I believed he could handle it.

"But what about the blood?" Vic twitched slightly, and he looked nervous. He was right. I had just offered to let my son babysit a potential killer. Whoever said stepmothers were evil?

"Vic, I know you're not going to like this, but we'll call my dad and have one of his deputies come over to be with Tyler," I said.

"Are they going to arrest her?"

"No. They're just going to make sure both of the people we love are okay. Is that fair?"

"I suppose that's the best deal I can broker in this instance. I'll be back just as fast as I can." Vic eyed Tyler. "Keep her here."

As Vic walked away, Tyler looked toward the house.

I put my hand on his shoulder. "You said you wanted us to trust you. Here's your chance."

We got to the church where a crowd assembled on the freshly-watered green lawn. It was midafternoon, and the summer heat was beating down mercilessly. There was a slight murmur among the crowd as they waited for the news of the winner.

Maggie and Ruby were standing near the back. "You made it," Maggie said with excitement in her eyes. "Did you find it?"

"No, it wasn't us, but we did find something, or should I say *someone* else. So, I'm guessing you don't know who the winner is?"

"Nobody knows. We thought it was you," Ruby said, fanning herself with her visor.

Heat and frustration had reduced the crowd of treasure hunters down to about half. I looked around, trying to take a mental roll call. If none of these people found the prize, then who did? As we waited for Rocky to emerge from the church with the winner, my father graced the steps. The crowd hushed as he turned to face us.

"Golden Pecan treasure hunters, there was a winner. But—"

"Who was it, Judd? It's too hot to stand out here and wait for you to get to it," someone shouted from the crowd.

My dad gave a brief smile. "I really hate to have to tell you this, but the winner was found dead just a little bit ago." A gasp went up from the crowd. Once more, I surveyed the gathered group of treasure hunters. Who was missing?

My dad pulled out his small black notebook, flipped it open, and began to read aloud. "Earl Brown found his brother Bosco dead at 3:45 p.m. in the basement of Benny's Barbecue, also the last clue location in the treasure hunt. Bosco Brown was holding the golden pecan when his brother Earl found him. Mr. Brown was the victim of a blunt force trauma. Now, normally, we would not give you this much information upfront but because emotions are running high with the treasure hunt, The Pecan Bayou Gazette and the chamber of commerce are calling off this year's event."

What my father didn't know was that Sarah Butler had been located, with fresh blood stains on her dress. I needed to get him alone right away.

Chapter 16

"What was the answer to the final clue?" Stan asked as he leaned against the red brick sign that read Pecan Bayou Community Church.

"That one was a real stretcher of our clue-finding abilities," Josiah said. "What was cold and dank?"

"Oh." My dad scratched the side of his head. "That would be the basement of Benny's

Barbecue. Frankly, I think it was a little underhanded for Rocky to choose a location that most people have never been in. The only way you could've figured it out was if you had used the facilities and even if you did, the cellar door said *Employees Only*. There was a tiny yellow arrow next to the restrooms pointing to the cellar door. No clue box, just the arrow. It was no bigger than a pencil, but I guess hunting for a big prize like this needs to be tough. That's all I have to say for now."

I knew all about Benny's basement. I had just helped Benny and Celia reorganize it. After getting strict instructions that we were not to go to the crime scene, most of the crowd milled over to Benny's with a sudden desire for brisket. The restaurant was still in operating order, but the restroom area where the door to the cellar was had been taped off. A deputy was posted in front of the area.

"Why are we here?" Leo asked as we walked into the crowded restaurant and found what looked to be the last vacant table.

"To find out what happened. Look around you. The rest of the town is here. Why not join them?" The string of jingle bells attached to the door rang incessantly as more treasure hunters crowded into Benny's restaurant.

"May we join you?" Maggie and Ruby now stood at our table.

Leo grimaced. "Why not? The more, the merrier. Besides, I don't think there's an empty table in the entire restaurant."

Maggie squeezed in next to me and then leaned over and whispered in my ear. "Have they brought Bosco up yet?"

"I don't think so. You know Art was out on a fishing trip today. He can't be too happy that he was called back for two murders."

Rocky came up to the table and made a scooting motion with his hands intending to share half my chair. "Word has it you helped Benny and Celia reorganize and redesign their cellar storage area. Unbelievably, your knack for straightening things might actually come in handy this time. Is there a possibility you could draw me the room? We could use the graphic in the paper."

Good old Rocky. We were shocked by yet another grisly murder, but he was busy planning the layout of the next issue of the Pecan Bayou Gazette.

"I guess I could." I grabbed a large white napkin and Rocky's pen.

"Let's see." I quickly scribbled out the details and labeled each area. "There's shelving on the right and then a turntable organizer in the middle. They have refrigerators on this wall and a freezer on that wall. Don't forget, the cellar has two doors. One in the restaurant and one that faces the alley for deliveries."

Rocky examined my drawing and pointed out a space between the organizer and the freezer. "That means whoever killed Bosco probably dropped him in this area."

Ruby put her zebra-striped fingernails on Rocky's arm. "Do we know who might have murdered him yet?"

"Not that I've heard, but the competition this year was pretty aggressive. Usually, this treasure hunt is fun. Goofy even. Whoever got to Bosco was violent. Benny's wife Celia said there was blood everywhere," Rocky said.

Maggie piped up. "You talked to Celia?"

"Well, I didn't get to hear everything, but she was so upset that they called out Reverend Dansby to come talk to her. I guess she came down the stairs to pick up more pickles when she found Earl trying to call 911 over the dead body of his brother."

"And still the million-dollar question is, do they know who killed him?" I asked.

"I haven't heard a name yet," Rocky said. "I hate to say it, but they always suspect family members first."

Earl had carefully kept the information about his brother being a convict secret from the town for years. Maybe he was embarrassed by his brother's prison record. I couldn't imagine he would want to kill him, but Earl's livelihood—really his whole existence—had been threatened by Bosco showing up on the scene. Earl had always been thought of as a trustworthy member of the town. Now it seemed we were lumping Earl in with his brother. That had to be a big concern for the local barista. There was a rumbling at the back of the restaurant as the cellar door opened. The crowd went silent. The paramedics rolled Bosco out completely encased in a black body bag.

"Why didn't they use the alley door?" Leo whispered.

"Mayor Obermeyer's truckload of water. It's still blocking the alley," Rocky said, reaching for his phone to snap a picture.

Behind the stretcher, Lieutenant Boyle came out with the object that had been the desire and focus of the residents of Pecan Bayou. The golden pecan. The sparkling gold glitter was now spattered by the dulling effects of dried darkening blood and encased in a clear evidence bag.

"I'll be back," I said.

"Where are you going?" Aunt Maggie said as I started in the direction of the bathrooms. "You know you can't use the restroom until they take down the crime scene tape."

"I know. I need to talk to Dad about something we saw."

Leo nodded. "Do you want me to go with you?"

"No, I think I can handle it," I answered as I reached for the crime scene tape in order to slip under it. One of my dad's volunteer deputies had been posted at the door, and his big frame loomed within it.

"Now Betsy, I know you think you got special rights at all your daddy's crime scenes, but I can't let you go down there."

"I know that, but I just need to say something to Dad. It won't take a minute." From the look in his eye, I could tell the man was thinking about it. "It has to do with the case. I might have some information that could help."

"What kind of information?"

"I saw someone in town covered in blood," I answered quickly.

He moved aside. "Don't trip on the stairs."

Even though the body was gone, there were still rivers of blood staining Benny's nicely resurfaced floor. A shaft of light came into the cellar from the door that was open to the street. Looking macabre against the creeping red puddle, a giant yellow banner had been hung from the ceiling tiles congratulating the winner of the Golden Pecan Treasure Hunt. There was a lingering scent of vinegar in the room. Some of the shelving Benny, Celia, and I had carefully planned and placed was now on its side along with jars of pickles that had smashed on impact. The glass crunched under my feet, causing my father to look up from his notes.

Dad stood with his hand on his chin, turning at my footsteps. "Betsy, what are you doing here?"

I would like to say he looked happy to see me, but it was just the opposite. Annoyed might be a better word.

"I'm sorry to bother you, Dad. I know how busy you are, but I needed to tell you about something that happened just before we came to the diner. We found Sarah Butler."

"Wonderful. That's one thing off my mind. I think that's the first good thing that's happened today."

Before he could celebrate his lightened workload, I added, "And she was covered in blood."

"Where is she now?"

"Tyler's sitting with her at her house."

"Did she injure herself?" he asked, still not making the connection with Bosco's murder.

"She didn't seem to be hurt."

"I see. Do me a favor and go ask Benny if Sarah had been in the restaurant earlier," he said, sending me back up the rickety wooden stairs.

Benny was working in the kitchen, turning ribs and giving out orders to the wait staff when I found him.

"Plate those and get them out to table five," he said to his son, Jerome.

"Benny," I said.

"I'm a little busy, Betsy."

"I was wondering if you saw Sarah Butler in your dining room earlier."

Benny, sweat on his brow, looked at me with frustration. "I don't know. Maybe. I've been too busy to notice who's sitting out there. They order food. I cook food. That's about all I've been doing. First, we're the only place open in town, and now we have a crime scene that every gossip in three counties wants to get near. It's crazy. Why?"

"Oh, nothing. Go back to the ribs."

Sarah could have slipped in, but why would she choose to go to the cellar? Could she have been in a dream state and stumbled down there thinking Bosco was part of the nightmare? It was a stretch to be sure. I texted my father.

With the contest now officially over, many of the participants were heading home. If there would be a prize, it would surely go to Earl.

"Well? What did you see?" Rocky asked when I returned to the table.

"Pickles."

Rocky started to write that down and then looked up. "Pickles?"

"Oh, and broken glass," I added. "There wasn't a lot to see. There was some blood, but that was about it."

"Well," Maggie said as she rose from the table. "I suppose that's a blessing. This old girl's tired. Let me get my son from your house. Time to make a fresh batch of sweet tea and put my feet up. Do you want to come over, Ruby?"

Ruby let out a sigh. "Nah. I think I want to be alone. I was sure we were going to win this year. Oh well, I suppose we can try again next year, but chances are the prize won't be as good as a cruise."

"I heard Lester Jibbets was thinking about donating something for next year," Rocky said.

"The Port-a-Potty king? Oh Lord, just one more thing to get depressed about." Ruby slung her bag over her shoulder.

"I'm heading home for a nap," Leo said in my ear. "Care to join me?"

As enticing as the idea was of curling up with Leo in the air conditioning and letting the day recede away, I decided it was time for some nice hot coffee. "You go ahead. I'll be there in just a bit."

Leo raised an eyebrow. "What do you have to do?"

"I promise, I won't be long," I assured him.

"Let her go," Maggie said from behind us. "I know that look, and it's best you let her get it out of her system. I'll go with you to pick up Danny."

Ruby let out a disappointed sigh. "Well, I guess I won't be hitting that cruise anytime soon. Such a shame, really. I just bought my first bikini in twenty years."

Leo held up a hand to stop the beautician before she went into any more detail. "Too much information, Ruby."

"What? I'm not ashamed of my body. It took years to get it to look like this." She did a little sashay with a Vanna White swoop at the end.

"I'd like to see you in that bikini," Lester Jibbets said as he came out from nowhere.

"I'm just sure you would, Lester, but I guess fate has stepped in, and I won't be going on any cruises," Ruby said, shutting him down quickly.

When I stopped into Earl's Java, I was surprised to see it was still open. Earl couldn't be waiting on customers after what had just happened to Bosco. There wasn't a soul in the store. I followed the sound of water and found Earl in the backroom scrubbing out a giant coffee urn. He wasn't just scrubbing the thing, he was taking the finish off of it.

"Earl, are you all right?" I asked gently.

"What do you think? My brother was just murdered. Someone in this town killed him, and you ask if I'm all right. Hell no, I'm not all right." He went back to scrubbing.

"Do you have any idea who might have killed him?"

Earl stopped again and mopped his brow, a line of sweat threatening to drip into his eyes. "Bosco had a knack of rubbing folks the wrong way. It could have been someone from his time in prison, his business dealings, or someone he crossed in the contest. What can I say? My brother was a real horse's ass. I guess he got that from our daddy."

"Earl?" A voice I instantly recognized came from behind us in the coffee shop. My father had come to question him. It was part of the standard investigation to grab the family members first.

Earl put down the plastic scrubber, rinsed the inside of the coffee pot, and headed for the counter. When I emerged behind him, my father gave me a curious look.

"I thought you'd be home by now." He gave me a look that didn't hide his annoyance at my meddling.

"I was worried about Earl, and I thought I'd check on him," I rolled off quickly.

"Uh-huh." Dad didn't look convinced.

"Did you talk to Sarah Butler?" I asked.

"I tried to, but it seems she's sleeping it off. Tyler had already left for your house, and Vic told me to come back later."

"Did he say anything about the blood on her dress?"

Earl picked up on that. "Blood? Do you think that woman killed my brother?"

My father cast a stern look my way. "That's nothing but pure speculation at this point, Earl."

"So, you don't know who killed Bosco?"

"Not yet. We were hoping you could help us with that. Do you mind coming over to the station?"

Chapter 17

I was a little surprised Dad didn't push Vic to let him see Sarah, or at least the bloody clothes. There was a little bit of a southern gentleman that made him step back to observe protocol, but still. How did he know Vic wasn't in the house looking up helpful hints to get blood out of clothing? It isn't hard. You just have to use a little hydrogen peroxide. After so many years following my father around, that little tidbit of information had come in handy more than once. I wrote that up years ago, and it was greatly appreciated by our local doctors and dentists.

I was also surprised that Vic, a man notorious for people-pleasing, actually said no to someone. Maybe everything that had been going on with his wife was changing him. He had to be feeling a loss of control with her wandering around the streets at night, both awake and asleep.

When I pulled up to Vic and Sarah's house, I was surprised to see smoke rising from the backyard. I ran through the wooden privacy fence as the smell of burning filled my nostrils. Flames rose up from an outdoor firepit. Vic threw a piece of clothing that I recognized as Sarah's red dress onto the flames. He was burning the evidence. This proved he believed that Sarah killed Bosco and would go to any length to protect her. Even destroy evidence.

I came closer to the fire. "Vic? What are you doing?"

"Betsy? I didn't hear you," his eyes darted to the dress, the stink of the polyester blend material wafting through the air.

"You're burning Sarah's dress? I thought you would want to turn that into the police. It might be part of a murder investigation."

"Don't say that. Of course, it's not. Sarah had a cut on her hand, that's all." I had held Sarah's hand and didn't remember any cuts.

"So why are you burning it? Why didn't you try to wash it out or at least throw it out?"

Vic shifted, and I could tell he was stalling as he tried to come up with an answer. "I told you, it's ruined. I don't see how any of this is your business." It seemed Vic's perpetually nice attitude had shifted to a definite chill.

"I'm sorry, it's just weird, you know. You have to admit it doesn't look good."

"You think I'm trying to protect my wife, and well, maybe I am."

"It certainly looks that way."

"You don't understand. She's...the most beautiful woman in the world. Not only on the outside but on the inside. Her soul is just as incredible as her body. When she agreed to marry me, I thought it couldn't be real, but she did. If you think I would do anything for her, then you are correct. I would."

"Even cover up a crime?"

"Of course not."

"You know I'm going to have to tell my father about your little fire," I said, thinking someone who would do anything to save their wife might also strike out at someone threatening to tell. Not my smartest move.

"I would prefer it if you didn't. I know this looks suspicious, but trust me, Sarah could never kill a man, especially in a sleepwalking state. I know I said she could be extremely dangerous, but murder? That's another thing all together."

"Can I talk to her?" I asked.

"No. She's still sleeping."

"Have you checked on her lately? How do you know she hasn't wandered off again?" Sarah had gotten by him before, why not now? I thought of Poppy Donaldson. "Was she really the one who pushed Poppy off the bridge? She kept talking about it."

"No." His voice, normally on the high side, took a little tonal leap.

"How can you be so sure?"

"Maybe she was talking about it, but that doesn't mean she pushed her off the bridge. She had been upset by the whole thing, and it evidently slipped into her subconscious. That's all. Now, if you'll excuse me, I had better go check on her. I will trust you will use discretion in this matter?"

"Uh, if you mean I won't let Rocky print you're burning a piece of potential evidence, then yes, I will."

"And your father and the murder investigation?"

"I can't promise anything. If your wife committed a murder, then I can't let that go by."

When I got back home, Maggie was still at the house working in the kitchen. Even though she had to be exhausted, she decided to cook a big supper. "I may as well cook it here rather than go home and just cook for Danny and me. Besides, after all that we've seen today, I want to be with the ones I love."

I was more than happy to let her indulge us with her wonderful home cooking. My refrigerator had been well-stocked, and she took advantage of that, whipping up sour cream enchiladas. As Aunt Maggie worked in the kitchen, I made sure that Coco cleaned up the mess she made in our absence, and with great theatrical pain, she began trudging back and forth to the toy chest, lugging Barbies that had to each weigh ten pounds. If Barbies were flesh and bone, there would be some major concussions going on.

Once I was sure Coco would finish her task, I found Leo. I wanted his take on Vic burning Sarah's dress.

"So, you're saying that you think Sarah Butler is responsible for two deaths?" Leo asked.

"I don't know, but as soon as we get the kids eating, I'm going to tell Dad everything, including seeing Vic burning Sarah's dress."

"I don't know, Betsy." His statement surprised me. Vic was clearly destroying evidence.

"What do you mean you don't know?"

"Look at this way. If she really is suffering from a neurological ailment, how can anything even be pinned on her? I mean, what is the legal precedent for killing somebody while unconscious?"

Aunt Maggie clunked a pan in the kitchen. We lowered our voices.

"I don't know what it is either, but that doesn't mean we can let this mystery go unsolved."

"Supper's ready!" Aunt Maggie yelled out two of the most important words in the household around five in the afternoon. Footsteps began tromping her way. Twenty minutes later, as we were just finishing up Aunt Maggie's delicious enchiladas, my father came knocking at the door.

"Well, this is a surprise," I said as he pulled up a chair next to Coco.

"I hear you have been in a bit of trouble lately, young lady." Now, most people would be a little unnerved when a policeman said that to them, but Coco just smiled at her grandfather as she held up a piece of food.

"No, I haven't," she said. He smiled at me.

"Well, I guess I'll just have to ask your mom about that and see what she says."

"No," she protested.

"That says it all, darlin.'" He laughed.

"Can I get you a plate, Judd?" Aunt Maggie asked.

"Now, that would be right nice." My father nodded and placed a napkin in his lap. "You'll be glad to know that I have Sarah Butler coming in to be questioned about the death of Bosco Brown. So, I can only stay a few minutes because Vic and Sarah are due to come to the station in the next hour. Did you want to tell me something about burning evidence?"

"How did you find out about that?"

"It seems my sister is very good at eavesdropping."

Aunt Maggie raised her hand. "Promise me you won't get mad, but if Sarah Butler killed that man, then she can't let her husband cover it up for her. It's just not right. I know you were going to go talk to your father eventually, but I wouldn't be able to sleep tonight thinking she's out sleepwalking looking to murder somebody else."

"What are you talking about?" Danny said as he came into the room. We had always tried to keep information that would upset Danny quiet, but this time he had overheard.

Maggie waved a dishtowel at Danny. "Oh nothing, baby. Everything is fine. You know I like to pick on Betsy."

Danny smiled. "We all like to pick on Betsy."

"Yes, well, I think you'll sleep fine tonight, Maggie," my father reassured her, rolling his eyes at his sister's antics.

Tyler, who had been listening to the entire conversation, finally spoke up. "Do you think she'll remember anything? I mean, when I'm in like a dream state, I don't remember anything. It's just bits and pieces when I wake up. It could be like that for Sarah."

I couldn't help but notice that Tyler was now on a first-name basis with Sarah Butler. Had she told him to call her Sarah, or was he thinking about her so much that his manners slipped?

"Well, I guess that's what I'm about to find out, son," Dad answered.

"Would you mind if I went down there too?" Tyler asked. "Just in case she needs moral support?" I hated to break it to him, but she had the moral support of a husband who would do anything to protect her, even lie to the police.

I tried to break it to him gently. "I don't know about that, Tyler. This is a murder investigation, after all."

Tyler put his hands together in front of him in a prayer-like position. "Please?"

Leo scooped an enchilada out of the pan. "I don't think it's a good idea."

Tyler, who was always quick on his feet, came up with another tact. "What if I have a parent with me? Then if I'm interfering, Betsy or Dad could bring me home?"

My dad drew out a sigh. It was not the first time he had been worn down by a persuasive grandchild. "I don't know."

"I'll go with him," Leo said.

"Don't go, Daddy," Coco said. "I want you here. You still haven't taught me how to ride without my training wheels."

It seemed Coco had a new person to badger about her bike lesson every hour. I wasn't surprised that she was choosing her father over me. Lately, I had been laying the law down to Coco on a regular basis. Daddy, on the other hand, could be a bit of a soft touch, as many fathers were, including my own. Rather than risk a temper tantrum, I volunteered. "I could go."

"Even better," Tyler smiled. "If you can't trust her own daughter, who can you trust?"

And once again, we had catered to the whims of a high school senior and a preschooler at the same time.

Chapter 18

A few minutes later, we found Sarah, Vic, and their lawyer, Ray-Ray Benning, sitting in chairs along the wall of the hallway to the interview room. Ray-Ray, although wild in high school, had turned over a new leaf and was now practicing law in town. I wasn't surprised to see Vic Butler bring a lawyer to a question-and-answer session. He thought his wife might be guilty. She was now dressed in a white t-shirt that was close-fitting and a pair of white and blue striped shorts that showed off her shapely legs. Even in casual clothes, she looked like a model for Dillard's.

"Betsy?" Vic said upon seeing us.

"Tyler wanted to come, to give Sarah moral support," I answered quickly.

"I'm here if you need anything, Sarah," Tyler's words were so sweet it left a lump in my throat.

She reached up and patted his hand, her blue eyes flashing to his. "Thank you," she whispered.

My father cleared his throat as he stepped out of the interview room. "You folks can come on in now."

Even though Tyler had wanted to comfort Sarah, it seemed the Pecan Bayou police force didn't keep people waiting long. I knew he would be disappointed, but we couldn't go into the actual interview. "Tyler just wanted to make sure Sarah was okay. We'll head home now."

"I'm not going anywhere," Tyler argued, planting his feet on the floor.

There was never a force so stubborn as a young man who thinks he's falling in love. "We can't go into her police interview with her," I said.

"I would like it if Tyler was there," Sarah said. She then acknowledged me. "You can come too, Betsy."

Vic bristled slightly. "Sarah, dear. They are questioning you about murder. You really want to invite half of the town in to hear all about it?"

Her eyes met his. "Just for a few minutes. Do you mind?"

"What do you think, Ray-Ray?" Vic asked.

"It is highly irregular, but if it makes my client more comfortable, then...what the hell?"

Vic drew in a breath. "If it makes you feel better, then fine. But just for a few minutes."

After we all found our places, we were each offered bottles of water. After that, Dad punched a digital recorder on the table and began to speak. "This is an interview with Sarah Butler regarding the murder of Bosco Brown. Now Mrs. Butler—"

"Call me Sarah."

"Sarah," he corrected himself. "Let me just start with the obvious. Did you have anything to do with the death of Bosco Brown?"

Sarah paled. Ray-Ray immediately put a hand on her arm and began to whisper in her ear. Then he faced my father. "She's choosing not to answer the question at this time. We are still unsure of what happened because of her illness and so to confess to something today would not be wise. We don't even know if she was there and if she was there, she doesn't know."

Sarah stared at her own folded hands. "When I get that way, I remember very little. I can see some faces and hear some voices, but everything is blurry like being in a fog."

"That's enough, dear," Vic said. "Judd here knows the information you give will not be consistent."

Vic unscrewed the top off a water bottle and took a slug. This interrogation had him sweating profusely, and stains were spreading under his arms. Instead of putting the cap back on, he laid it on the table. It reminded me of my boys. At the end of a heavy day of playing video games, I would find a slew of water bottles and caps everywhere.

My father looked perturbed. "Okay. So, what you're basically telling me is because you were in a sleep state that you really can't answer any questions? Do I have that right? I'm not even sure why you came in. It is also unusual for a person to come in with their lawyer right off the bat. Speaking from the perspective of a policeman, it does make me a tad bit curious."

"We do hope you can understand why we have chosen to have legal representation at this questioning," Vic said. "We want to do anything we can to cooperate, but until we know my wife's true state of mind at the time, there isn't any point in answering questions. I hope that's okay with you."

That had to be the nicest explanation of why a suspect planned not to cooperate with the police that I had ever heard. Once again, Vic had smoothed things over for his wife. What I wasn't sure of was how long he could keep doing that. Sarah was literally the smoking gun, or should I say the bloodied dress.

"And that tells me I don't have a choice," my father continued. "Even though you cannot remember things because you may or may not have been asleep during the murder, it doesn't mean that I will not continue to dig through evidence. I hope I've made that clear." From the tone of my father's voice, I could tell his patience was running thin with Vic and Sarah Butler.

After Sarah, her husband, and lawyer left, my dad leaned on his elbows, resting his chin in his hands. "Well, that didn't get us anywhere."

Tyler crossed his arms. "I don't even know why you're questioning her. She obviously didn't do it. She has a sleepwalking disease. You needed to be nicer to her, Grandpa."

Dad gave him a grin. "You think so, do you?"

"I think you have a little crush on her," I said.

Tyler blushed a deep red. "No, I don't." His words pierced the air proving I had touched a nerve. Dad and I exchanged a look. Neither one of us believed him.

When we returned to the car, we found Belinda Donaldson writing a ticket and placing it under the windshield wiper.

"We haven't been here over two hours," I said, pulling the ticket back out.

Belinda swallowed slightly as if I were a bad taste in her mouth. "No, ma'am, but you did park in a space that's reserved for police cars."

Pecan Bayou was too small to have a parking lot dedicated to city vehicles, so the town council had opted to reserve a space in front of each municipal building to accommodate the people who worked there.

"But I'm Judd's daughter. I'm part of a police family."

"Do you work at PBPD?" She tilted her head slightly and widened her eyes.

"Well, no, but—"

"Then, this discussion is over. I can't get over how some people in this town think they're special just because their daddy's a cop."

I guess she didn't give much credence to blue pride. I took the ticket and stuffed it in my bag. "Fine."

"Fine," she repeated, walking down the street to find someone else's day to ruin.

Tyler didn't speak to me the whole way home. I was grateful for the silence because it gave me some time to think about the death of Bosco Brown. Bosco had been an obnoxious man who was way out of bounds in his methods to find the golden pecan. Ironically, when he finally did find it, someone killed him. Now whether or not they killed him for the golden pecan, or they killed him because he was such an obnoxious man, we might never know. Whoever the murderer was, they were still walking around the streets of Pecan Bayou, feeling like they had gotten away with something. They might feel like they had done our town a favor getting rid of such a criminal. Could it be the killer was cleaning up the streets of Pecan Bayou vigilante style? The idea of someone out there thinking they were allowed to kill people because they might be suspects in a crime was frightening to think about.

If Bunny could alibi Sarah, who was on the bridge, and Sarah could alibi Bunny, who was under the bridge, who killed Bosco? Of course, Sarah did show up in a bloody dress. The next question I would ask would be how long Bosco had been dead in the basement of Benny's Barbecue. I quickly ran through the list of contestants who were fighting with Bosco over the prize. There wasn't one of them that I felt had so much invested that they were willing to murder him for it. It also didn't work out with the death of Mark Valencia. Once again, I was bouncing back to possible vigilante justice occurring in our town.

Who in town was so stuck on right and wrong? As I glanced over at the ticket that now stuck out of the top of my purse, Belinda Donaldson's name came to mind. Since she had taken over the role of the meter maid, I never left my car for more than an hour anywhere in the downtown area. She loved to chalk those tires, and if she came back, I would get a ticket for sure. Ruby said that she had collected fourteen tickets on her yellow Jeep Wrangler, and it had been parked in front of her own beauty shop. Belinda was a woman with a cause, that was for sure. Drifting back to my ideas on vigilante justice, I decided the killer hated wrongdoers, and Sarah Butler seems to figure prominently in each situation.

Also, the murderer was very good at slipping in and out and not leaving any evidence.

If all that was true, then I would need to somehow involve Sarah if I wanted to catch the killer. It would need to be something not fair. I didn't normally gossip, but this time I would use gossip as a weapon. When I saw the lights on at The Best Little Hairhouse in Texas, I pulled into a parking spot. Tyler shot me a look.

"Aren't we going home?"

"Sure, I just need to stop in here for a minute."

"Fine, I'll just walk home. It's only three blocks anyway." Tyler unsnapped his seatbelt with a jolt and exited the vehicle, striding down the street in anger. Why did I get the feeling this was going to be the world's longest senior year? You look forward to your child graduating from kindergarten on, and then you meet the adolescent version of that apple-cheeked angel.

When I stepped inside of the beauty shop, I was surprised to see Ruby sitting in a black styling chair downing a Lone Star beer.

"Hello, Betsy. Have you come to my pity party?" Ruby asked as she guzzled some of the golden brew.

I took a seat in a second chair, resting my feet on the metal bar that served as a footrest. "Come on, if you really wanted to go on one of those singles cruises, what's stopping you? You don't have to win a prize to go on a cruise."

Ruby's focus was in the mirror as she began to peel off a fake eyelash. Now that false eyelashes were all the rage, I noticed that Ruby had started wearing them sometimes, hers complete with small sparkles at the end. If there was a beauty fad out there, Ruby was always glad to add her own spin to it.

"I suppose you're right. I must have some room on one of those credit cards. How am I ever going to find Mr. Right when I'm stuck in this place surrounded by post-menopausal women? We haven't had an eligible bachelor move here in years." She took another swig. "Sorry. This really is a pity party. I'm just tired. Really tired."

"I know, and it doesn't help that we've been around two murders today. Every time something like this happens, it just makes me sad that someone would do this to another person," I said, priming the pump.

"That's for sure," Ruby said.

"I've been working on some theories," I said.

Ruby finished off the last of her beer and tossed it into the trash can, causing a clunk that echoed across the walls of the empty salon. "I'm listenin'."

"Here goes. Sarah Butler is much more involved in this than we might've thought. I also think Sarah might've had something to do with illegal goings-on at Maximum Muscle. Whoever the killer was, they were very into taking the law into their own hands."

"Just like Dog the Bounty Hunter. Now there's a handsome guy, but he needs to get rid of that screamin' shade of blond dye in his hair."

"Who?"

"Don't worry about it."

"Okay. Then absolutely," I continued.

"I'm listening. What have you got up your sleeve, Houdini?"

"Right now, I feel like I'm fresh out of tricks."

"You know, I heard that Belinda Donaldson is glad that Mark Valencia is gone so she can open a yarn store over there," Ruby said.

"Really?"

"Yes. She had dibs on that site before he moved in but couldn't leave her job until June. By that time, Mark had signed the lease for Maximum Muscle."

"I didn't know that," I said. "She couldn't have been too happy about it."

"What do you think? She was livid."

"Was she angry enough to kill Mark?"

"Belinda? I'd be very surprised if she could go that far. Those Donaldson girls have always been high strung. I blame that on too much granola. Still, though, they don't seem like a pack of killers."

"I don't know. I just feel like I'm missing something and that if I can get just one more look at Maximum Muscle, I might figure it out."

"Like what?"

"I have no idea. If Belinda takes over the space, maybe she'd like for me to come in and straighten that place out. You know, help her organize Mark's inventory to ship out to wherever. That kind of thing."

"There you go with that junior detective stuff again. Here I am looking for excitement, and all I really need to do is follow you around. Everybody knows Belinda and Bunny eat at Birdie's every Saturday night. You can talk to them there."

"Thanks, Ruby."

She answered with a slight belch.

"What do you want?" Bunny said as I approached their booth at Birdies. The three Donaldson sisters used to sit in the far booth by the window watching the foot traffic in downtown Pecan Bayou. Poppy would sit next to the window on one side, and Bunny sat on the other. Belinda always sat at the far end of the booth and usually took care of ordering for the family. Now that Poppy was gone, her space by the window was vacant. The remaining sisters looked a little sad sitting in their accustomed places.

"If you're here to fight that ticket, you're wasting your time." Belinda took a drink from a tall red plastic cup and returned her gaze to the window.

"I actually wanted to talk about your yarn shop."

Belinda put the cup down and began tearing the napkin that was taped with paper around her silverware. "What yarn shop?"

"Come on, Belinda. Half the town knows you wanted the retail space where Maximum Muscle is now. Not that being the town's most successful meter maid isn't fulfilling, but I think people around here can't wait to have an outlet for needlecrafts. May I sit down?"

"If you must," Belinda pointed to the empty space next to Bunny.

"Now, you got yourself interrupting our dinner," Belinda said. "What are you proposing exactly?"

In the corner of my eye, I saw Bunny scooting away from me and moving closer to the window. Birdie arrived with the sisters' plates. Bunny had the salad, but Belinda had the chicken fried steak. Not what I expected from a person who lived with the owner of a natural foods store. From what I could tell, Bunny might be pushing her opinions on people like Rocky and me, but when it came to her sister, she knew when to shut up.

"Have you read Marie Kondo?" I asked.

The sisters answered me in unison. "Who?" Their voices sounded as if they were one person in stereo.

"You know," Birdie said. "That little woman who runs around saying *spark your joy*. She has a documentary streaming right now." Surely they had heard of Marie Kondo? The woman was changing lives.

"Who the hell is that? Does she live around here?" Belinda asked.

"Marie Kondo," I repeated. "The organizing guru?"

Belinda flipped a wave in the air, brushing off the importance of knowing about the organizing pop star.

"Whatever. Get to the point."

I scrambled for words. I was losing my audience. "I want to volunteer to help you organize your new store. It's part of what I do."

"Oooh," Birdie interrupted. "I'd love it if you'd do it for the diner. Silas, our cook couldn't find the flour yesterday, and we had to go buy pies."

"If it means keeping this town stocked in homemade pies, I'd love to help out," I answered, making Birdie smile.

Belinda took a bite of her heavily breaded chicken fried steak and squinted her eyes. "Now, why would you want to do something like that if I did open this yarn shop? I don't have any money to pay you."

"And I'm not asking you for any. I just get a lot of joy out of reorganizing things. You know I just did the cellar at Benny's Barbecue."

"You mean where they just found a body?" Bunny asked.

"Yes, unfortunately. It was so sad about Bosco Brown."

"Right. Sad. Were you related to him in some way?" Belinda asked.

"No."

"Good. I wanted to know if I was insulting a relative. He was nothing but a piece of prison trash. Probably got what was coming to him."

"Wow. You really have a bad opinion of him. Did you know him?"

Belinda's chin rose. "I gave him a parking ticket, and he threw it right in my face. I know people don't want to get a ticket, but you don't need to attack me. I can't help it if you all want to willingly break the law."

Things really had changed for Belinda since the entire downtown parking territory became an issue for every merchant on the street. Before this, she simply marked the cars in the courthouse parking lot, and that was plenty. Now she had the entire city angry with her. It was tough to be Belinda Donaldson.

Birdie placed a hand on her hip. "I don't know if throwing tickets warrants a man's death. He was overbearing, that's true but so are a lot of people."

Belinda smoothed a mound of mashed potatoes across her steak. "I say he got what he deserved along with that muscle guy."

This was getting interesting. Not only did she have a grievance against Bosco, but she didn't like Mark. Two victims, two connections.

"Did he throw tickets back in your face too?" I asked, trying to keep it light but hoping she would blow up a little and let more information out.

"No. He wasn't my problem. He was Poppy's," Belinda answered.

"Enough, sister. You talk too much. Her father is a policeman," Bunny warned.

"What was going on between him and Poppy?" I asked.

"Yeah, what," Birdie echoed.

"You don't have to answer that," Bunny said.

"Be quiet, Bunny," Belinda said. She turned back to me. "Let's just say when a person likes to fish at night, they may or may not see criminal behavior occurring."

"She saw Mark break the law?" I asked.

"She did?" Birdie repeated.

Belinda squirmed at the sudden barrage of questions. "She saw something. We're not sure."

"Do you think whatever it was figured into her death?" I asked.

"Enough," Bunny said. "You're holding up our dinner."

Belinda took over. "All right, Happy Hinter. I don't know why you're doing it, but I got permission to go through the store tonight and take measurements. You can meet me there and give me your ideas. Lester Jibbets owns it. I guess making money on tiny poop houses wasn't enough for him. Now he's buying up the downtown area. Who knew there was so much money in portable toilets?"

And now, I had permission to get back into the store and keep searching for clues. "I'll be there. You know, I love the detail, and I think I might know some things about what happened to Mark."

"Like what?" Birdie asked.

"I'm not totally sure, but I always say the best way to find something is to start cleaning. I wonder what I'll find while cleaning up Maximum Muscle?" I answered. Belinda watched me for a moment but then went back to her dinner. Bunny slid me a look that I wouldn't call friendly.

Birdie looked around the diner. "I should get back to work." She rushed off to another table to take their order and relay the latest news.

Chapter 19

"Let me see if I can get this straight," Leo said. "You're telling me you have arranged to meet with Belinda Donaldson tonight in order to gather more clues in an investigation that your father is working very hard to complete. Why are you doing this?" Leo was not at all happy that I had planned this rendezvous with Belinda Donaldson on false pretenses.

"Maybe I'm just doing a good deed. After the death of her sister, it's only right to be nice to her."

"Uh-huh." This was Leo's polite way of telling me he did not believe a word coming out of my mouth.

"I just want to get one more look at the place. I might pick up on something that would lead me to the killer. No matter how many times I go there, I feel like I've missed something."

"And you had this discussion in the middle of Birdie's Diner?"

"Everybody knows they eat there every Saturday night. It just turned out that way." Leo might not know all the facts, but he was an intelligent man. Yes, I was putting myself at risk, but with all my insane need for order in my life lately, this felt like a dirty plate left on the counter.

"I don't know Betsy. Nobody knows who killed Mark or Bosco. Maybe you should just stay here at home where it's safe."

Tyler came down the stairs in his sock feet and went directly to the refrigerator. "You should know by now your wife has an insane desire to fix everything." He slammed the refrigerator door shut and ran back up the stairs.

"Well, I guess I know now that Tyler is still angry with me," I said.

Leo put his arm around my waist and pulled me closer. "He'll get over it. The Fitzpatrick man you need to worry about now is me."

I held up two fingers. "I promise. I can take care of myself." As he pulled me closer, my elbow hit a plate of cookies on the counter, knocking them to the floor.

As Leo lowered his lips to mine, I pulled away. "Let me just get that."

"Sure."

"I guess I'm pretty excited about quitting the meter maid business and opening up a yarn shop," Belinda said as she searched for the key.

"You know what you're going to call it?"

Belinda fiddled with the key in the lock. "I was thinking about Belinda's Balls. You know for balls of yarn, but Bunny seems to think that people would laugh at that."

I stifled a giggle. "You know how people are today, picking up on every word. How about something like Belinda's Basket of Joy?"

"Maybe. It seems a little long for me. I guess it will come to me." As the key clicked in the lock, Belinda opened the door and flipped on the light.

When I entered Maximum Muscle, the store still smelled of the sickening sweet strawberry vitamin mix. Maybe Bunny had been right that building muscle should be organic, not chemical. The nighttime serenade of the frogs as they greeted the sunset was loud enough to be heard through the closed windows. After my intense Marie Kondo training, I was excited to think about putting in an organization system at the beginning of an endeavor. Mark had a well-kept store, but I noticed no one had taken out the trash and there was a distinct odor of decaying chicken coming from the tall white kitchen trash bag. It might have been left by Mark or it might have been left by Boyle when he was posted at the scene. Either way, it had to go.

My heart leapt through my chest when there was a slight tapping on the door. Leo pressed his face against the glass.

"Who is that?" Belinda asked.

"My husband."

"Why is he here?"

"What can I say? He worries too much."

"About what?"

Leo tapped again. "Let me in."

As I opened the door, he said, "Did you think I was going to let you do this by yourself? Are you crazy? There have been two murders in this town, and you want to go back to one of the crime scenes to spread your organizational love? What woman in her right mind would want to do this?" His gaze switched from me to Belinda. "Hello."

"Yeah," she said, not gracing him with a return greeting. "As long as you're here, hold this end of the tape measure. I'm going to try and build a counter to fit here."

Leo gave a quick nod and took the end of the tape measure.

I had to admit being married to me could be a struggle sometimes. I was also pretty darned glad that he showed up. "What about Coco? Who will put her to bed?"

"The boys can handle it."

I wasn't sure how I felt about him leaving our daughter in the hands of two incredibly distracted babysitters. We had been gambling on the attentiveness of adolescents all day, and nothing seemed to be improving. "You know they forget to read to her."

"She'll just have to miss a chapter of Junie B. Jones tonight."

"You're right. I guess it's not such a big deal if we miss one night."

"Stand over there," Belinda said after writing down a number. Leo obliged and changed his position. Belinda noted the number when she reached her second measurement but began scribbling with her pen. "That's the end of that one. I need to go to my car anyway. I brought some catalogs for store equipment. I want you to take a look at them, Betsy. Be right back." She took the end of the tape measure from Leo and returned to the street.

Once she was out of earshot, Leo said, "So have you figured out what you might be missing?"

"Not yet. There probably isn't anything, but I can't stop feeling like the answer will come to me here."

"Even with Belinda around?"

"Actually, I'm not sure if the killer might not be Belinda. If it is her, it will give her a chance to pounce."

"What? Come on, let's go."

"Come on, Leo. This isn't some kind of rabid killer who knows all. You're being paranoid. We're just here helping Belinda and giving my thoughts a place to formulate."

"I don't often do this, because I think of our marriage as a partnership, but get your purse. We're going home. This is much too dangerous for either of us. I don't know if you caught onto this, but no one has ever called me 'Dwayne the Rock' Fitzpatrick. Neither one of us is prepared to tackle a killer."

Once again, there was a tap on the glass. To my surprise, Ruby Green stood there as she waved with her synthetic fingernails.

"What is Ruby doing here? Hasn't she followed us around enough today?" Leo looked a little disappointed.

I opened the door. "Hi there," Ruby said. "I know you probably don't need any help, but I thought maybe I could help you…organize. What do you think? I keep my stock of beauty products pristine. I'm pretty good at this tidying up business even if I haven't read that woman's book."

I felt a warm glow. Ruby was there to protect me. I wasn't quite sure how much help she could be, but she had come to my rescue once before. It was just the fact that she thought she could that made me love her even more.

"Come on in," I invited her.

"We were just leaving," Leo said.

"Leo thinks I'm putting myself in too much danger with this being a crime scene and all."

"Posh. You're not in any danger, especially with someone like Leo."

I cast a sideways look at my "Dwayne the Rock" Fitzpatrick.

"Besides that," Ruby said, "we're here to clean up this place so that Belinda can open up a yarn store. If she's selling skeins of yarn, then maybe her replacement as meter maid won't be such a stickler for timed parking. I'm going to have to have a perm sale to pay for all those parking tickets. Who knows? Maybe I'll to take up knitting. Maybe it will satisfy me more than a singles cruise."

"You don't understand what Betsy's true purpose for being here is," Leo said.

Ruby smiled. "Of course, I do, dear."

Just as I was about to put my opinion in, there was another, much stronger knock on the door. "It's me, Bunny. I'm here to help you properly dispose of this toxic waste. Let me in."

I went to the door and opened it, and Bunny marched to the middle of the store. I looked to see if Belinda was right behind her, but Bunny had driven up in her own car. "If that's product from the store, you just can't throw this stuff in the trash. Who knows what kinds of toxins and evils this garbage has in it?"

"Come on in," I said. "Belinda should be back in just a minute. She ran out to her car. Now, before you get too excited, all we're doing is measuring tonight. You don't have permission to start throwing bottles against the wall."

Bunny harrumphed. "If you say so. I still think this whole place needs to be wrapped up and left at a toxic dump. When will people realize eating a healthy diet will give you everything all these powders and pills offer."

"I think we should all go home," Leo said.

Bunny looked confused. "Why? This cleanup needs to happen. Even if we're not doing it tonight and have to wait for this guy's relatives to show up and pack this stuff up, we can at least make inventories of what he has for proper disposal."

"I care a lot about our planet, or I wouldn't be a meteorologist, but we can do this during the day. I don't think it's safe here."

Bunny looked around the store. Then to my surprise, she agreed with Leo. "You may have a point there. This place reeks with bad karma."

"Thank you," Leo said. "I say we all leave together as soon as Belinda returns."

I grabbed the trash bag I had already filled. "I'm going to take this out to the alley. The trash pickup will be in the morning, and I don't want to miss it. Besides, we don't want to leave it open because of the odor."

"Let me take it," Leo said.

"It's not heavy. I can get it."

I hurried out the door to the alley. The sun had gone down completely now, and there was very little light except for the faint drift of glow from the streetlights several feet away. As I lifted the dumpster lid and attempted to hoist the heavy bag, I heard footsteps behind me.

"Can I help you with that?"

Vic Butler took the bag out of my hands and tossed it into the dumpster, carefully replacing the lid.

I gasped. "I didn't expect to find you back here."

"No. I suppose that you didn't."

"We were just helping with some clean up but decided to do it tomorrow."

"That was very nice of you. I admire your community spirit."

"There isn't much to clean. Mark Valencia was a pretty tidy guy. You know, I've been to the store several times, and I found one drawer open and an old coffee cup. That's about as messy as he got."

"Interesting. Whose coffee cup did you find?"

That was a strange question. Why would he ask that? Wouldn't he assume a cup would have belonged to Mark, the store owner? And then it clicked. "You."

"Excuse me?"

"You put Bosco's cup in the store."

"I beg your pardon? Why would I do that?"

"I'm not really sure...yet." Vic, the ex-rodeo cowboy, bank president, and all-around hero of Pecan Bayou. He was married to the beauty queen. The only thing I could find wrong with him was he was messy. He didn't close cabinets or put the cap back on the water bottle. I had a feeling if I went into his bathroom, I would find the cap off the toothpaste. "You know, I've been seeing your trail everywhere, but never connected it to the murders. For some reason, you killed Mark Valencia. You also killed Bosco."

"I think you've had a long day, Betsy. Maybe you should go home and forget we ever had this conversation."

"No. I think I've finally figured out why I needed to come here. It was the drawer that was opened. Mark wouldn't have done that, but you would. You're forgetful. Messy, even."

"My, my. You are the observant one. I guess I'm just a messy guy. Lucky for me, though, you are the only one who is tuned into those fine details because you're some organizational ambassador. Frankly, I couldn't care less. I have bigger things to worry about."

"I'm actually surprised you're messy because you always seem so regimented in your work."

"When it comes to my profession, I am very regimented, but sometimes I just like to kick back. I'm not a geek all the time. Not unusual."

"Was it tough for you?"

"What?"

"Being married to such a beautiful woman. She gets prettier every year, but you are starting to look a little weathered."

"Thank you, I think. I'll admit I got incredibly lucky when Sarah agreed to be my wife. I would do anything to protect her."

"Even lie about the fact that she has something to do with Poppy Donaldson's death?"

"Even that."

"So why did you kill Mark Valencia?"

He gave me a cold grin. "He was walking by the bridge that night. Swears he took a cell phone photo of what happened. He wanted money. Lots of it. I guess when you work at a bank, people assume that money in the vault is yours. That was why I really had you searching this place. I needed to find that phone."

"You mean you killed him because he was blackmailing you? What if I had found the phone and found the pictures?"

"Like I said, I would do anything to protect my Sarah. She's fragile. I can't have her going to prison."

"You think she killed Poppy?"

"I'm not sure, but it's not a chance I was willing to take."

"So, you killed Mark because he could implicate your wife?"

"You see, Mark had been following her that night. He was a rather strange man who likes to take pictures on his cell phone. Sarah was in one of her sleep states, and when she rushed at Poppy Donaldson, knocking her off the bridge to her death,

Mark got it all on video. That was when he began blackmailing me. I had to kill him. He refused to turn over the video file."

"And Bosco Brown?"

"It appeared Bosco didn't have two brain cells to rub together, but somehow he figured out that I killed Mark Valencia. Apparently he showed up to visit Mark just as I left, after I killed Mark. Bosco said he'd keep quiet if I told him where the golden pecan was. But that would be cheating and so unfair to the good people of Pecan Bayou. I will not have anybody cheat in my contest."

"And that was when you lured him to Benny's basement?"

"Yes. I waited for Bosco, and when he came down the stairs, I threw him the golden pecan and then rushed him with a fire extinguisher I found placed upon the wall. You really did a nice job down there, by the way. His head split open like a watermelon. He didn't even know what hit him. You'd think a guy who had been to prison would have quicker reflexes than that."

Vic sighed. "Oh well. Some people are such a disappointment, don't you think? I had found Sarah by that time, and she saw me kill Bosco. Of course, she was in a sleep state and tried to protect Bosco. That's how the blood got on her dress. She picked him up from the floor and held him in her arms. When I tried to get her away from him, she slipped out of my grasp and ran out the back steps to the alley. I needed to make sure I hadn't left any fingerprints. When you called, I was just starting to look for her."

My head was spinning with all the double standards that Vic Butler was handing me. If it had anything to do with protecting his Sarah, then it was okay by him.

"Now that I know all this, what are you going to do about me?" I asked. Vic knew I was going to run to the police just as soon as I found a way to get myself out of this situation. I had to find a way to keep him calm.

"Yes. Sometimes I wish you were more like Sarah. As beautiful as she is, I found her easy to control. Unfortunately, your strength is not in beauty but intellect."

"Then you should know I'm smart enough to keep my mouth closed. I'll give you time to get away. That's the best I could do."

"Are you kidding me? We both know you are lying. I'm sorry, but you should have stuck to writing your little column and let all this alone. I'm afraid you can't straighten this out, Happy Hinter."

"That may be, but there is a little detail you have accounted for. You're always missing the little details. I am not alone. Leo, Ruby, and Bunny Donaldson are all in the store right now waiting on me and Belinda's out here somewhere looking for something in her car. She may be watching this whole scene and dialing the police right now."

Vic glanced toward the store and then took hold of my arm.

"Then we'll just have to do this somewhere else won't wait. Won't we?" Putting his hand over my mouth, he began to drag me out of the alley.

Chapter 20

I screamed as hard as I could but couldn't make enough sound to let the people in the store hear me. Bunny was going off on some topic having to do with the environment her raised voice ruining any chance of them hearing me. He put an arm around my neck, covered my mouth, and dragged me out to his car that was parked on the side street. Pushing me into the back seat, he slammed the door. As he rounded to the driver's seat, I pulled on the handle, but the door didn't open.

"Childproof locks. What a wonderful invention. You may as well make yourself comfortable."

"Where are we going?" I asked as Vic took off down the street. All the while, I began to calculate if I could get over to the front seat without wrecking the car. A drop of sweat dripped off his temple. This was the first I'd ever seen him sweat. Even in the torturous heat of the contest, he always seemed cool and composed.

With his eyes never leaving the road, he answered, "To my house, of course. You don't think I walk around with murder weapons, do you? I'm a little more civilized than that. Just like a small business loan, this kind of thing takes planning and patience. Be patient, Betsy."

I was glad I would have more time to stall with the hopes that someone would find me, but I didn't relish the idea of him going home to find a weapon to use on me. I tried to keep the conversation light.

"What about Sarah? Did you say she was at your house?"

He gave a confident smile. "Sarah won't be a problem. I made sure she had more of her sleeping medicine before I left. She'll sleep through the whole thing." He snapped his fingers in the air as if having a "eureka" moment. "Better yet, I might tell her she did it. She'll need a lot of comforting when she finds out what a monster she is."

"You act like you've done this before."

"Do I?" Even though he was sweating profusely, his tone was light as if I had just told him he had a speck of lint on his shirt. This was what distinguished a normal man who committed murder to a man who thought committing murder was normal. Vic was in the latter group.

Vic pulled into his driveway, put the car in park, and turned off the motor. He then turned back to me. "You're not going to give me any trouble, now are you? This murder thing is getting easy. You would hate for me to take out your lack of cooperation on another family member after I finish with you. Trust me in this, you really don't want to make me mad. That's what happened to Mark Valencia. I never would have slit his neck with that bottle, but there was just something about him that got under my skin." He started to giggle to himself. "I guess I got under his skin too."

As Vic put his hand on the door handle, I began to run through escape strategies. I could attempt to scramble from the back seat to the front the minute he exited the car. The chances were, he would be there to grab me in the front seat. I seriously doubted I was faster than him. No, if I were going to escape, it would have to be after he opened the door. Because Vic must've known I was planning my escape, he opened the door quickly and grabbed my arm so hard I was sure he disconnected it from my shoulder.

"Let's go." He pulled me up to the steps with his hand over my mouth to muffle any screams that might alert neighbors.

Once inside, he threw me into a chair and grabbed a cord out of a lamp.

"I've never liked this lamp. One of Sarah's finds. Such a shame it broke." He began to secure me to the chair, and my several escape plans were narrowing down to nothing. Securing the last knot, he leaned in, close to my ear. "Now, you sit still here, Betsy. Let me just go to the kitchen and pick the perfect instrument. It's lovely having the luxury of picking something instead of grabbing the first thing I can find. I'll be sure to shut the drawer this time. Oh, and I'll probably need some trash bags. Getting dirt out of this carpet is a bear. Of course, you already know about that kind of thing, don't you? Back in a flash."

He danced off to the kitchen. He was going to enjoy killing me. He was beginning to like killing people. As I sat there, I realized I was way out of my league trying to find a killer. Why would I ever think I could outsmart somebody devious enough to get away with murder? The problem was no one suspected him, and they couldn't imagine that I was sitting tied up in the house of the president of the chamber of commerce. Vic had complimented me on my attention to detail, but in this case, like an errant sock or an unfolded shirt, it had slipped by me. Somewhere, sometime, I lost control of the situation. I never really had control even though I fooled myself into thinking that I did. Surely Leo must've checked the alley by now. I was surprised he hadn't shown up before Vic nabbed me. But of course, once Bunny got on a subject, it was hard to step away.

In the distance, the sound of metal kitchen utensils rattled in a drawer. Vic was looking for the perfect murder weapon. I tried to focus on my escape. I pulled my wrist to see if I could free myself from the lamp cord hold. After several tries, I surmised, Vic must've have used a cow securing knot because nothing was moving. I could try to bounce the chair to the door, but then how would I get the door open? That would also produce enough noise to alert him. The last thing I wanted was for him return any faster.

"Vic," I yelled out. "You don't want to kill me, Vic."

"Oh, yes, I do," he assured me, his cheery mood still evident.

"Pssst." Sarah stood at the door with one finger over her lips. "Don't let him know I'm here." I was able to read her lips, and I nodded. I had never been so happy to see her.

Vic entered from the kitchen with his hands behind him, hiding whatever instrument of torture he had chosen. I only had to hope Sarah had gotten out of his line of vision before he entered. My heart was beating so fast I worried I would die from a heart attack before he could kill me.

"You're so cute. *You don't want to kill me, Vic*," Vic said, mimicking my voice. His appearance had changed dramatically. He had removed his shirt and slipped over a shiny green trash bag with a hole cut out in the top for his head. He also had several more trash bags stashed under his arm. Vic Butler didn't intend to leave any evidence.

"You're actually trying to reason with me? Talk me out of murdering you because I'm a fan of the Happy Hinter? I read your column every week. I don't always agree with it, and some of those recipes seem a little far-fetched. Still, though, there's not much more to read in that paper, and you did help me get that irritating stain off my toilet bowl. I guess you can go to your grave feeling good about that."

I know he was trying to help me feel better, but really? He had his hands behind his back, but then his smile widened, and he lifted one arm up into the air holding a butcher knife. As the overhead light glinted off the polished blade, he moved around me, going from side to side as if judging the best place to insert a knife.

I saw movement at the window. I was grateful the outdoor spotlights allowed me to recognize the form of my stepson, Tyler. I was also grateful Vic was focused on his plan to kill me and had his back to the window. What was Tyler doing here? He could get hurt—or worse. Tyler held up his phone and backed away from the window. I didn't know why he was there, but even with my reservations I couldn't have been happier to see him. I hoped his gesture meant he was calling the police.

I glanced discreetly toward the doorway. Sarah was no longer no longer there. My heart began to race. Vic could actually get away with this, but I know he wouldn't do it until he put the trash bags around me on the floor. I hoped and prayed Sarah would do something to stop him in the few seconds that might remain in my life. Visions of Leo and the kids, Danny, Aunt Maggie, and my father flashed before my eyes. Would this be it? Would Coco have to grow up without a mother the same way I did? I could try to capsize the chair before the knife came down. It was a dangerous gambit because once I was defenseless on the floor, there was no moving out of his way. Vic was carefully arranging the trash bags around my chair on all sides.

"There we go. Don't need to have blood sinking into the floorboards. Those pesky crime scene investigators can find it anywhere these days. It's so important to be careful."

"You know, before you get started with this job, and I'm sure it's a big job for you, you aren't as neat as you think you are."

Vic's eyebrow rose. "Excuse me?"

"You missed a spot. Blood would seep in over there. Possibly, this might work better if you overlapped the trash bags. That way, if blood slips off one trash bag, it will simply go to the one underneath it."

At first, Vic looked confused as I pointed out this little flaw in his pre-murder planning. Then he started to get angry. Not exactly the emotion I was trying to evoke in a man who was dead set on murdering me.

"You know what your problem is? You spend your whole life trying to correct people. Does it make you feel good to always be right? Who cares?"

"I care," Sarah said, her voice clear and very much awake. She had a revolver pointed directly at Vic.

Vic looked like someone had yelled "surprise" at his macabre killing party. "Sarah, my dear. You need to put the gun down. Do it for me, darling. Please don't kill anybody else" He turned to me. "It's the medicine. She's dreaming. She won't remember a thing later."

"That's where you're wrong," she said. Her hand was shaking but she kept the gun pointed at Vic. She looked even more frightened than I felt. "I didn't take the medicine. You see, when I was in and out for the last day or two, I started remembering things. I started remembering how Poppy Donaldson went over the bridge. It really was my fault. That's the thing about having your eyes open—the memory still registers. You just have to dig to find it. I also know I had nothing to do with the deaths of Mark or Bosco. That was you. You told me all about it as you sat by my bedside, thinking I was asleep. That was some sick bedtime story."

Vic still stood with the knife held up in the air as if he were some sort of town statue. Would he now consider killing both of us? I hardly thought he could kill the woman he loved so deeply, but now that she knew what a monster he was, it changed things.

"You know why I did it. It was love. The purest love that a man can feel for a woman. I did it all for you, my darling. What we have here is perfect, and they were going to get in the way. Can't you see that? No one can love you the way I do."

Sarah wavered a bit. "Stay strong, Sarah," I said. "He's done everything he can just to keep you here. He's told lies about you. He told lies to you to keep you here."

Her doe-like eyes widened. "You lied to me? You lied about me? How long has this been going on? How long, Vic? That isn't love. That's evil."

The tableau between husband and wife was chilling. He, with the knife raised above his head and her, with the gun, fully extended and pointing toward him.

Would they kill each other, leaving me trapped in this chair, surrounded by their dead bodies?

"Let me just take care of this loose end, and then we'll sort all this out, sweetheart. You're upset."

I was the loose end.

"I'll finish up here, and then we can make a nice dinner and talk. Communication is the key to any successful relationship. Don't you agree?"

It sounded like he was quoting an article out of Redbook. I was so glad they were communicating, but why did I have to die in the process?

Sarah stood straighter, planting her feet slightly apart. "You need to put the knife down, Vic. It's all over. You may love me, but I could never be in love with a murderer. Killing people is the exact opposite of loving. You took those men's lives because of me. Do you think I will ever sleep again because of that? Do you think I could ever sleep next to you again? What you did was horrendous, and it has to stop. Put the knife down." Her tone had changed. It was low and even, and she meant business. Her hand stopped shaking.

"You're confused, sugar. Trust me in this. It's better for everyone. If I get arrested, if I go away, who will take care of you? You would be defenseless. You know you have problems," he reasoned.

"What about this woman's children? What about this woman's husband? Is it better for them? Did you ever think about how your actions affect other people?" she countered.

This time Vic did not come back with a condescending answer. He emitted a growl. "You obviously don't understand. This nosy woman means nothing to us. This situation is her own fault. Curiosity killed the helpful hints writer. Just go to upstairs and lie down a bit. I'll be done in a minute."

"I'll shoot you before you can stab her. Don't think I won't."

"How can an angel kill someone? It is not in your DNA, sweetie. It's okay, I'm going to keep you safe." He turned back to me, raised the knife, and began to swoop toward my chest. Before he could make contact, the deafening sound of the gun went off in my ears, and Vic Butler, president of the bank and head of the chamber of commerce, crumpled to the floor. She meant what she said.

The police, and Tyler, burst through the door in the next instant. My father rushed to the body of Vic Butler, but instead of going to Sarah, Tyler ran to me and began to untie my hands and feet.

"Thank God you're all right." There were tears in his voice. "I came over to check on Sarah, but no one answered. When I looked in the window, I saw you sitting here, and there was nothing I could do. I didn't know what to do."

"You did the right thing. You called your grandfather." I reached up and hugged him as he began to sniffle. "You saved me, son. I don't know what I would've done without you." Tyler's arms tightened around me as he sobbed. Yes, he was becoming a man, calling the police proved that, but at this moment, he still needed the comfort of a mother.

Chapter 21

Birdie's Diner was overflowing with customers now that it had reopened after the contest. Aunt Maggie and Ruby had commandeered a booth and had placed their bags on the seats to discourage anyone else from joining them. Danny sat on the end seat, leaning on his elbow as he watched the comings and goings of the town.

I scooted in next to Maggie. "Have they said anything yet?"

"Not yet, but everybody and his uncle is here. Birdie ran out of chairs, and she can't keep up with coffee refills."

Rocky, holding a piece of paper and looking very official, unseated one of the diners and stood on his chair. "Can I have your attention, please?" This was it. The big moment we'd all been waiting for. What was going to happen to the coveted golden pecan and the money that went with it?

"Well, this is definitely a golden pecan treasure hunt that will go down in history. Sadly, because of the murder of Bosco Brown, we did not have the opportunity to award the cruise to anyone. His brother Earl has expressed no interest in the prize."

"He doesn't deserve it," someone shouted out from the back.

"I think you're all wrong about that. Yes, Earl was the brother of Bosco, who was an ex-con, but Earl is clearly the victim in all of this. I think he's being right kind saying someone else should take the money. I also think this town owes it to him to support Earl's Java during this troubled time. Don't stop going to Earl to get your coffee. He not only needs your money in his till, but he needs to know that he still has friends in Pecan Bayou. What do you say, folks?"

Whoever it was who had spoken up in back was now silent. Many eyes were cast downward, probably considering Rocky's declaration. He continued, "Now we had a lot of thoughts on this. We could try to rerun the contest, but I know that it takes a lot out of everyone. We really didn't have anyone in second place, so Libby Loper and I came up with a solution."

Libby rose from her table and stood next to Rocky, her turquoise jewelry and fringed vest looking particularly smart today. She nodded her approval at Rocky and held up a coffee can.

Rocky took it out of her hands. "We've decided to let you vote on who you think should get the prize money."

"Hot dog. How do you spell R – U – B – Y," Ruby whispered.

Rocky smiled. "You can vote for yourself, sure, but is that what our little town is all about? No. We can't stop you from putting your own name down, but we want you to dig deep in your heart and think if there was someone else who deserves this prize more. This needs to be another contestant who was running the race. Someone you know deserves and needs this vacation or prize money. I've always been told that it is better to give than receive. Keep that in the back of your mind as you fill out your ballot."

Once the ballots were passed out, I quickly scribbled a name on it and folded it up, waiting for the coffee can to come back around. Maggie and Ruby did the same, as did Leo.

"Who did you vote for?" Leo asked.

"I'm not telling. It's a secret ballot."

"Me either," Leo answered.

"I just have to say I'm so glad they caught Vic Butler. In a million years, I never would've thought he was the—" Ruby looked over at Danny. "A bad man." Ruby knew not to discuss things like murder in front of Danny.

"Nobody did," I said. "Everybody loved Vic. He was so loving toward Sarah and a friend to a lot of ranchers around here when they needed a loan at the bank."

Leo held up a finger, "Yes, and he got something that most men never get. The prettiest girl in town. He also found out how much work it is to have such a beautiful woman on your arm."

I jabbed my elbow into his side.

"Of course," he corrected. "I also know what it feels like." The ladies around the table laughed.

"They have also reopened Poppy Donaldson's murder, or should I say accident? Do you think they will charge Sarah Butler?" Maggie asked.

"I don't think so." I said. "It really was an accident, and once she started remembering, she remembered it all. They found Mark Valencia's cell phone and the video he took of her that night on the bridge. She was in a deep state of sleep and thought that Poppy was a monster. She was fighting for her life. She threw the monster over the bridge, and Poppy hit her head. It's strange legal ground."

Ruby clucked her tongue. "I saw Bunny down there by the banks of Pecan Bayou planting more flowers. You know she actually waved and smiled at me? Something about her has changed. Maybe just finding out how her sister died made all the difference. She's helping Belinda open the yarn shop. Of course, she's insisting on sustainable yarn. But that's okay, she's not running around town like a pot about to boil over. As awful as all of this was, I think it helped Bunny."

Birdie came by, and we dropped our ballots in the coffee can and then went to the front where Rocky and Libby began to count out the vote. It was only a moment later when they returned with the results.

"We have a winner. Many of you voted for this team, which shows just what a wonderful part they are of our community. I am happy to announce that this year our beloved Prim Thatcher and her husband Josiah will be going on a cruise in the beautiful waters of the Caribbean. Congratulations."

Josiah and Prim rose from their table as the crowd gave them a hearty round of applause. I couldn't think of a better team to win the prize.

"I guess our romantic cruise is off," Leo whispered in my ear. I suddenly remembered a scene from *It's A Wonderful Life* where Mary Bailey put up travel posters for the honeymoon destination they would never get to see. "You know we don't need a ship to rock the boat," I said.

Chapter 22

"Betsy, where are my socks?" Tyler yelled down the stairs.

I'd been anxiously awaiting this question. I couldn't wait to tell the boys how much easier their lives were going to be with my latest organizational effort.

"I moved them. I've created a sock and underwear area in the top dresser drawer. I think you will find that if you can just roll your socks and t-shirts neatly you will have much more room in your dresser. Isn't that a great idea?"

Tyler grunted and raised both hands in the air, palms toward me. "Betsy, please. You have to stop. You're driving us all crazy with this stuff."

Zach, who had been in his room upstairs, came out. "What's going on? I'm trying to get through that summer reading list Mom gave me. I'm almost to the top of the rocket ship." I thought it would be inspiring if I listed his book titles on the body of a rocket ship and even put the words Read to the Stars underneath it. I thought it was quite clever.

"Of course you are," Tyler said. "She has reorganized every door, every closet, every cabinet, and none of us can find anything. If always tidying up is supposed to make life better, why are we are all so miserable?"

"I was just trying to find the joy." I was sure that reminding him of my mission statement of tidiness would slow down his outburst, but Tyler was on a roll now. All that pent-up frustration seemed to be aimed right at me.

"Is finding the joy micromanaging every inch of our lives? You set up a schedule for my sports practices. If I'm a minute late, you're texting on the phone. You have to stop. I'm almost a man, but you're treating me like a three-year-old."

"He does have a point, Mom," Zach said. "You've taken this tidying up thing just about as far as it can go. I don't think you have to work this hard to find joy."

That was it. My whole family was now against me just because I tried to improve their quality of life.

"Fine. You guys just go ahead and live in the mess that you create every day. Find your own socks. While you're struggling, I'll have my own neat area where everything is organized and easy to find." I grabbed my keys, slung my purse over my shoulder, and headed out the door. How could they not appreciate what I had done? This was homemaking taken to the next level. The expert level. They were lucky to have me. A tear began to roll down my cheek as I pulled into the park, where I knew Leo had taken Coco to play. I found a seat on a park bench. Butch, happy in the sunshine, was running in circles. Leo had taken him off his leash, but he seemed perfectly content to stay in the park. Our sweet Weimaraner bounced up to me and then put his head on my lap. I was grateful for the company. Why was it that dogs instinctively knew when you needed a friend?

There was a slight breeze today, so the heat had subsided. I sat back and let it drift over me. When I heard a squeal, I looked up suddenly. I hadn't realized that Leo had brought Coco to the park with her bike. I thought she was just playing on the playground. Not only that, he had taken her training wheels off. She wasn't ready for this yet. What was he thinking?

I had wanted to take this step-by-step. Maybe make a motivational chart for the refrigerator. This wasn't something to go into it willy-nilly. She had been badgering me for weeks, but I had been hesitant, especially to take the training wheels off her bike. Leo tried to convince me this morning that it was time to do this. I had visions of multiple Band-Aids and possibly a bandage wrapped around her head after getting a concussion, but Leo assured me that he could teach her to ride a bike. She wasn't ready. I wasn't ready. Once she started riding her bike, it was only a couple of steps until she was in school, and then the years would go by too fast.

They stood at the edge of the park sidewalk, the summer sun and azure blue sky framing them in an idyllic picture.

"Okay. You have your hands solidly on your handlebars?" Leo asked.

"Yes, Daddy," Coco answered, a little perturbed.

"And what do you do when the bike starts to wobble?"

"Try to center the front," she answered, as if reciting a Bible verse. It was obvious Leo had tried his best to instill some safety guidelines into our daughter. I had to give him credit for that.

"And you know that if you start riding by yourself really well, I'm going to let go. That means you will have to use your brakes to stop. Can you do that?"

"Yes, Daddy." She was losing her patience with him. As terrified as I was of the next step, she couldn't wait.

It seemed like just yesterday she was a baby. Now she was getting ready to tear up the sidewalks with her bike. It was the same way with the boys. I could still remember Zach trying to break a Guinness world record using rubber bands when he was little. Had it been so long ago when Tyler was worrying about starting middle school? They grow up so fast, and no amount of organization can stop it.

"Okay, here we go."

Coco began to pedal. The fringe on her pink boots was awfully close to the chain on the bike. Leo should have changed her boots, but it was too late now. She was on her own. They began to run across the park on the sidewalk. Butch took off to join the bike ride, his low bark echoing behind her, cheering her on.

An enormous grin spread across Coco's face. "I'm doing it, Daddy. I'm doing it. Let go. Let go."

Don't let go, I thought. *Whatever you do, don't let go.* She gained more speed, and Leo took his hand off the back of the bike. My heartbeat spiked. This was it. This was the moment when she would go out of control, I thought, but instead, she soared across the playground sidewalk, the smile remaining on her face. My little girl had found her joy. She found it without fringe-free boots or training wheels. I was amazed. Maybe it was okay sometimes just to let something fly. Maybe I didn't have to keep trying to straighten out the world. My thoughts stopped abruptly as I began to worry whether Coco would be able to stop the bike. She was going at a terrific speed and was coming to the end of the park sidewalk. The brakes squeaked as she pulled her feet back to stop. Coco had made a successful first run. She turned the bike around and shouted for everyone in the park to hear, "I did it! I can ride a bike."

Leo yelled back, "You did it!" Butch barked and jumped in circles around Coco.

I ran over. "Great job, Coco."

"Mommy! I did it!" She hugged my waist.

Leo joined us. "I know you wanted me to wait, but sometimes we just need to let go."

His words sank into me. He was right. I needed to let go. Tyler didn't need his schedule to be laminated and put on the refrigerator. Zach didn't need his reading list to be written on a poster of a rocket ship. Sometimes tidying up too many things can actually *kill* the joy.

I put my arms around my dear Leo as we watched our beautiful daughter glide around the park. There was no denying it.

It sparked my joy.

Helpful Hints from the Happy Hinter

Turning Plastic Bags into a Waterproof Doormat

1. Cut plastic bags into ½ inch strips. You are creating "Plarn" (Plastic Yarn).

1. You can crochet (9mm hook) the strips together to make a waterproof doormat.
2. To join ends of strips, if you pull the plastic tightly it will minimize the size of the knot.
3. Chain the stitches you need for the length of rug you are making.
4. Row 2- Chain 1 and turn. Single crochet into each loop.
5. Continue making rows until your rug is the size you want.

Cheesecake Cookies

½ cup butter, softened
3 ounces cream cheese, softened
9 Tbsp. sugar
1 cup flour
¾ cup pecans, finely chopped

Combine butter and cream cheese. Add sugar, then flour and mix well. Scoop out one teaspoon of dough, dip into milk, then roll into a ball. Place balls on a foil-lined cookie sheet. Press balls flat to make thin round cookies about 1 ½ to 2 inches in diameter. Sprinkle with finely chopped pecans pressed lightly into cookies. Bake at 350°F for 10 minutes.

Yields: approximately 2 dozen cookies

Sour Cream Enchiladas
1 ½ lbs. ground meat
1 15-oz. can chili (no beans)
1 pkg. dry enchilada mix
½ cup picante sauce
1 tsp. garlic powder
2 lbs. processed cheese, grated (Velveeta recommended)
8 flour tortillas
1 Tbsp. chili powder
1 tsp. minced onion

Brown ground meat and onions in a skillet until the meat is no longer pink; drain. Return the beef and onions to the skillet and mix in canned chili, ½ of the package of enchilada mix, picante sauce, garlic powder, and chili powder. Simmer for ten minutes. In the meantime, prepare the sauce.

Sauce
1 stick butter (1/2 cup)
4 Tbsp. flour
½ cup milk
1 carton (8 oz.) sour cream

Melt the butter in a saucepan. Whisk flour and milk together, then pour it into the melted butter, whisking well to combine. Whisk in the sour cream and approximately 2 tablespoons of the meat mixture.

To assemble, spoon meat mixture down the center of a tortilla; top with cheese. Roll up and place in a casserole dish sprayed with nonstick cooking spray. Continue with remaining tortillas. Sprinkle the top with more cheese. Pour sauce over the top and cover with foil.

Bake at 375°F for 20 minutes or until sauce is bubbly and enchiladas are heated through.

Celia's Ginger Muffins

1 ½ tsp. baking soda
¼ cup hot water
1 cup sugar
¾ cup oil
3 eggs
1 cup molasses
1 cup buttermilk
3 cups flour
1 tsp. salt
1 ½ tsp. ground ginger

Topping

½ cup orange juice
¼ cup lemon juice
½ cup sugar

For Muffins: Dissolve baking soda in hot water in a bowl or measuring cup. Set aside. In a large mixing bowl, mix oil and sugar; add eggs one at a time, mixing well. Add molasses, then alternately add dry ingredients, buttermilk, and baking soda water, mixing well after each addition.

For Topping: Combine all ingredients in a small saucepan. Bring to a boil and cook for 4 minutes then brush onto cooked muffins as directed.

Fill greased muffin cups 2/3 full and bake at 375°F for 10-12 minutes. Brush tops of cooked muffins with topping and put under a broiler for a glazed effect.

Yield: 12

Don't miss out!

Visit the website below and you can sign up to receive emails whenever Teresa Trent publishes a new book. There's no charge and no obligation.

https://books2read.com/r/B-A-FJQD-HCGHB

BOOKS 2 READ

Connecting independent readers to independent writers.

Did you love *Die a Yellow Ribbon*? Then you should read *Oh Holy Fright*[1] by Teresa Trent!

Read more at https://teresatrent.com.

1. https://books2read.com/u/mVQ2Pr

2. https://books2read.com/u/mVQ2Pr

Also by Teresa Trent

Pecan Bayou
A Dash of Murder
Overdue for Murder
Doggone Dead
Buzzkill
Burnout
Murder for a Rainy Day
Till Dirt Do Us Part
Oh Holy Fright
Die a Yellow Ribbon

Piney Woods
Murder of a Good Man
A Sneeze to Die For
Die Die Blackbird

Redbird Creek
The Con Man's Daughter

Watch for more at https://teresatrent.com.